"Drake, what did you just do?"

Drake rubbed his chin, a frown on his face. "Uh, I kissed you."

"Yeah, you did. Why did you do that?"

"Because you wanted me to."

His answer was so matter-of-fact that she backed up a step. How the hell did he know that? "You can't just keep kissing me like that. You did it in Vegas, too. Just kissed me for no reason."

"You were upset, and I wanted you to feel better."

"So you kissed me?"

He sighed, rubbed his forehead. "I don't know. It just felt like the right thing to do at the time."

"And today?"

"I don't know," he repeated.

Love's curiosity got the best of her and she asked, "And how do you know I wanted you to kiss me?"

He shrugged, shoving his hands into his pockets. "I can't describe it. I can always tell when a woman wants me to kiss her."

"So you just do it?"

"Of course not."

"In this case you did."

"It's you. I kissed you because you wanted me to."

Dear Reader,

Dr. Lovely Grace Washington burst into my life one morning in 2010 while I sat with my mother in the hospital. The name struck me like a bolt of lightning, and I pictured a beautiful, successful resident doctor who couldn't stand her name and demanded everyone call her "Love."

I spent so much time at the hospital that I couldn't help but be intrigued by the lives of doctors. They devote so much time and energy into their work, and I wanted to give them a little happiness.

If you've read an Elle Wright novel, you've met Love in one of my previous books. Although she played a small role, I couldn't help but want to tell her story. Since I love a good friends-to-lovers story, I figured her best friend would be perfect for the headstrong Love.

I'm a graduate of the University of Michigan, and I love bringing readers into Ann Arbor and Southeast Michigan. I'm elated that you've joined me on this journey!

Love,

Elle

ElleWright.com

@LWrightAuthor

IT'S
ALWAYS
BEEN
You

Elle Wright

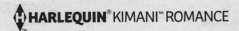

HARLEQUIN® KIMANI™ ROMANCE

Recycling programs
for this product may
not exist in your area.

ISBN-13: 978-1-335-21651-9

It's Always Been You

Printed in U.S.A.

There was never a time when **Elle Wright** wasn't about to start a book, already deep in a book or just finishing one. She grew up believing in the importance of reading, and became a lover of all things romance when her mother gave her her first romance novel. She lives in Southeast Michigan.

Books by Elle Wright

Harlequin Kimani Romance

It's Always Been You

To my mother, Regina. You are missed.

Acknowledgments

I thank my God for His protection, His provision, His love. I would be nothing without Him.

To Jason; my children, Asante, Kaia, Masai; and the rest of my family—I love you all BIG. There are so many of you, I can't name everyone. But you know who you are. I learned long ago that you don't have to be blood to be family. That couldn't be more true. I appreciate the time, the talks, the hugs, the tears…everything. I thank you all for your unwavering support.

To my agent, Sara—I thank you for believing in me.

To Shannon Criss, Glenda Howard and the Harlequin Kimani Family— I feel so honored to be a part of this extraordinary family. I dreamed of being a Harlequin author one day, and that dream came true.

Speaking of dreams, I still have to pinch myself sometimes. This writing journey has been amazing. I've met so many wonderful authors and readers. I feel so blessed. Thank you all for accepting me and encouraging me. You all mean the world to me!

Chapter 1

Dr. Lovely Washington frowned when she felt the sun beaming down on her. Morning already? She patted the mattress, pausing when she felt cool skin under her palm. Drake. She pinched him. He pushed her hand away, grumbling something incoherent.

She smacked him. "Drake, what are you doing in my bed? And please…close the blinds. The light is killing me."

"Whashuleafmelone," he mumbled.

"I won't leave you alone until you get up and shut out the sun," she said, pinching her forehead. "My head hurts. And aren't you late or something?"

When he didn't move, she went to throw the sheet off, then stopped abruptly. Frowning, she patted her bare breasts. Uh-oh. *Where is my shirt*? Reluctantly, she slipped her hand under the sheet, over her stomach, her belly button, her—

She sat up abruptly. "Oh, my God, I'm naked!" Her mind raced to remember how she'd ended up like that. Last night was a blur. They'd booked a two-bedroom suite at the Bellagio because her family reunion was there. Two rooms, two beds. Yet Drake was in her bed and she was naked. "Oh no."

Drake had agreed to come because she hated going to these things by herself, and she wasn't particularly thrilled to face her family alone after her breakup with Derrick. When she needed someone—and she did—Drake was always there. He was her very best friend, since the age of two.

Her night had taken a turn for the worse when she'd received a call from the hospital that she'd lost a patient. Drake had dragged her out onto the Strip to distract her. That was all she remembered.

She held her face in her hands, praying the shooting pain in her head would stop. She remembered something else. Tequila. Lots of it. Peeking through her fingers at Drake, she sucked in a deep breath. She couldn't tell if he was naked. He was lying on his stomach, his bare back gleaming at her in the sunlight. The sheet was draped low. Gently, she lifted the thin material.

"Drake!" she screeched, digging her nails into his back.

He pushed himself up on his elbows. "Ouch! What?"

"Get up," she ordered through clenched teeth. "Now."

He blinked and glanced at her with one eye. "What happened?"

Pulling the sheet with her, she hopped out of the bed. "Look at you," she said, pointing at his bare ass. "You're naked! Oh, my God."

"Oh, shit." He rolled out of bed onto the floor with a loud thump. Reaching up, he pulled the balled-up comforter with him. He finally stood up with the thick cover wrapped around his waist.

There was no movement—just eyes on eyes, heavy breathing and loud thoughts.

"Why are you naked?" Her heart raced as she watched his gaze drop to the bed.

Drake ran a hand through his wavy hair. "Why are *you* naked?"

She swallowed past a lump that had suddenly formed in her throat. "I asked you first," she croaked.

"Obviously, I don't know." He rolled his eyes and pinched the bridge of his nose.

"Why are you nervous?" she hissed. Drake was normally a calm and collected person, but they'd been friends long enough that she could recognize when he was nervous. After all, they'd been best friends for almost their whole lives.

His bloodshot eyes flashed to hers and his forehead creased. "I can't remember. I just remember walking on the Strip doing shots."

"What do you mean you can't remember anything? You're naked!" she shrieked.

He pressed a hand to his temple. "Love, please, be quiet. You're making my head hurt worse. I don't need continuous updates on our lack of clothing."

She clutched the sheet to her chest. Tears pricked her eyes. "Drake, did we…?"

He held a hand up. "Don't say it. There has to be a good explanation."

"But we're both…" She dashed a tear off her cheek.

"Don't cry. That's how we got into this situation in the first place."

Placing her hands on her hips, she hissed, "What the hell is that supposed to mean?"

He covered his eyes. "Pull the sheet back up, Love."

Realizing she'd let it fall to the floor, she screamed and scrambled to pick it up, twisting the fabric around her body. "This can't be happening."

He motioned toward the bathroom. "Put some clothes on, for Christ's sake. This is already bad enough."

"Don't tell me what to do."

"Go in the bathroom," he demanded.

"You go in the bathroom," she countered, clutching the sheet in her palms.

"Love."

"What?"

He stalked toward her and she retreated until the back of her knees hit a chair. Overcorrecting, she stumbled into the seat.

Drake held out a hand and she took it and let him pull her to her feet. Then she shoved him away. "Get away from me, you ass."

He nudged her toward the en suite bathroom. "Look, get dressed. We're never going to figure this out standing here like this."

"I hate you," she growled as she stomped into the bathroom. Kicking the door closed, she leaned against it. A hotel robe was hanging on a hook and she snatched it and slipped it on. Once she secured the tie, she whipped the door open and stormed back into the bedroom toward a now clothed Drake.

His back was to her and he was murmuring curses to himself. She jumped on his back and wrapped an arm around his neck. "You took advantage of me." With her other hand, she yanked his hair.

He fumbled with her weight and they both crashed down on the mattress. She flailed her arms and kicked at him until he grabbed her wrists and pinned them to the bed.

"Calm down," he pleaded. "Stop trying to fight me." The vein on the side of his temple jumped and his biceps bunched as he held her arms above her head.

Love was angry, but she was something else, too. Something that she'd never felt before. Well, tried to never feel before. His hard chest pressed against her soft one made it kind of difficult not to feel aroused.

"Get off of me, Drake." Needing to put some distance between them—because the last thing she needed was to be aroused—she bucked against him.

"Love, would you just…" He sighed, his hooded bedroom eyes boring into hers. *Bedroom eyes*? Her stomach fluttered and a warmth spread over her. She cursed her body for responding in ways she wouldn't dare admit.

Is he doing this on purpose? His eyes stayed on hers, seeming to look straight into her soul. Maybe he wasn't *trying* to turn her on, but he was.

"Promise me." His husky voice seemed to light a fire in her belly. "If I let you go you have to keep your hands to yourself."

"You took advantage of me," she muttered, her voice shaky. The anger she felt was melting under his gaze. Unclenching her fists, she let the tension ooze out of her arms. She chewed on her bottom lip. His breath fanned across her mouth and she couldn't help but entertain the idea of *letting* him take advantage of her.

"We don't know that," he said, snapping her out of her thoughts. "Neither of us remembers last night. You can't say for sure that we did anything but sleep."

"But we were naked," she murmured. *Why am I whispering?*

He squeezed her wrists. "Stop saying that. Let's concentrate on the present."

"Well, get your *naked* chest off of me and I'll try."

He jumped up, leaving her splayed across the bed, angry with her body for betraying her and with her mind for its wayward thoughts. She glared at the textured ceiling and prayed for a time machine that could zap her into yesterday, where Drake was merely annoying— not annoyingly sexy. Would she ever be able to look at him as the friend he was without thinking about his mussed hair and lean physique? Let alone the fine line of hair that trailed down his stomach and disappeared under the waistband of the low-riding sweatpants he'd donned. She tightened the belt on the robe and sat up, smoothing her hair back.

"What *do* you remember?" he asked, in the tone he often used on his patients. Detached.

Obviously, he wasn't as affected as she was. *Ouch.* She cleared her throat. "Lana called. One of my patients went into labor and was admitted to the hospital, possible peripartum cardiomyopathy," she answered, as if she was reporting to her chief resident during rounds. "Instead of paging me, she had paged Blake. The mother insisted on a natural birth, but her heart couldn't take the labor. She died. I was upset that I wasn't there, so you took me out to get my mind off of it."

He lifted his eyes toward the ceiling and muttered a string of curses. "I keep replaying last night over and over in my head. I can't remember how we got in bed. I remember the bar, the shots. You were finally loosening up. When we left Caesars, you were tipsy, so I had to kind of hold on to you. I can see us laughing at random people on the way back to the room. Then we ran into a few of our high school classmates. They asked us to go out with them, but you didn't want to, so we headed back here. Then..." He averted his gaze, swallowed roughly.

She bowed her head and wondered what he'd just remembered. They were friends. Best friends, in fact. They'd grown up finishing each other's sentences. Love knew all of Drake's "tells" and was certain he'd just filled in some blanks.

"The bar and walk I remember," she croaked. "That's about it."

It wasn't a complete lie. She'd been very inebriated, inconsolable over the loss of her patient. Drake had done what he always did—make it better, help her forget.

"Hopefully, it'll come back to us later. For now, we can't assume anything happened."

They'd shared the same bed many times during their lifelong friendship, and nothing had ever happened. Not even an accidental brush of arms. Hell, he'd seen her in her underwear plenty of times. But...

"We were still clearly on our own sides of the bed," he continued, without meeting her gaze. "There's no clue—"

"I feel sore," she blurted out. "My whole body does."

"You were drunk. You could've fallen or something."

Love wondered when Drake had turned into Mr. Positivity. The proof was staring them right in the face. The bed. She scanned the rest of the room before zeroing in on the bed again. Frowning, she walked closer to it and ran a finger over the tiny bright red spot. Closing her eyes, she gasped. "Oh, my God!"

"Stop saying that," he said, between clenched teeth.

"It's blood. There's your clue. We had sex."

"Love, you're not a virgin. The blood is probably from a paper cut or something."

"You don't really believe that, do you?"

He glared at her. "Just...be quiet. Let me think."

"You know we had sex," she muttered under her breath. And the worst part? She didn't remember the details. If she was going to participate in something that would more than likely ruin her friendship with Drake, she would've liked to remember it.

Chapter 2

Drake had a headache. And it was getting worse by the minute. He peered down at the tiny speck of blood on the stark white sheet. *Shit.*

The evidence was there. They'd woken up in bed together naked, she'd admitted her body was sore, and now there was visual proof. Not that he needed it. He knew exactly what had happened between them, but he couldn't say the word out loud. The memories were coming fast and furious with each passing minute, with her standing in front of him in nothing but the hotel bathrobe.

"What are we going to do?" she asked, sitting on the edge of the bed.

"Nothing." He cracked his knuckles, rolled his neck and plopped down next to her. When she scooted away from him, Drake tried to tell himself that he wasn't bothered. "We just have to deal with it. It happened."

She twisted the tie of the robe around her fingers. "I know we have two bedrooms, but maybe you should move into a separate room for the remainder of the trip."

He hated this. Love was his best friend. They'd spent countless hours together, shared many a hotel room and even a bed—platonically. He'd never thought anything else about it—until now. "What's that going to prove? Apparently, we've already seen everything there is to see."

"That's not funny."

It wasn't; he knew that.

"What if…it happens again?" she whispered.

His eyes snapped to hers. "It won't. I'm never drinking with you again."

She lowered her gaze. "You don't have to say it like that," she mumbled.

"How am I supposed to say it?" he asked incredulously. "You're my home girl. We've never done anything remotely close to this."

"We can't say that anymore," she muttered under her breath.

They exchanged glances before turning away. "I guess not," he agreed.

"I hope this doesn't affect our friendship."

"It won't." As much as he hoped it wouldn't, the very conversation they were having indicated that it might. Theirs was a relationship of comfort as much as it was one of respect and unconditional love, not marred by the hurt feelings and expectations that often accompany a love affair. Now, he couldn't even make eye contact with her—a fact that didn't go unnoticed.

"You can't even look at me, Drake."

"Neither can you," he retorted.

Love sighed and stood up. "Maybe I should just hop in the shower."

He rubbed the back of his neck. "Maybe you can soak in the bathtub," he suggested. "It'll help with the soreness."

Without another word, she walked into the bathroom and closed the door. Once he heard the lock click, he fell back on the bed. As he listened to running water, he ran a hand down his face. He needed Advil and quickly.

They'd had sex. But something didn't seem right. What had made this time different from every other time? Why would they choose this trip to get busy? The sight of Love clutching the sheet against her breasts for dear life haunted him. She was scared and teary-eyed. He closed his eyes tightly, hoping to erase the image.

He hoped the bath would relieve her anxieties. Deciding to take a shower himself, he slid off the bed and walked into the second bedroom. The Bellagio was Love's favorite hotel in Vegas and she'd insisted on splurging on the suite. There was a separate living room and two bedrooms—one for each of them. His en suite had a steam shower and hers had a soaking whirlpool tub.

He padded into the bathroom and turned on the shower. After waiting for the steam to fill the room, he stepped in. He placed a hand on the tile and let the water beat against his back, loosening his tense muscles.

His hand massaged her back as they burrowed into the mattress. Their lips touched in the softest of kisses. She caressed his face as he suckled on her bottom lip.

Drake shook his head as if to shoo away the vivid memories, and lost his balance. When he reached out to grab the bar, he slipped on the shower floor and landed on his ass. So much for relaxation. Taking a deep breath, he sat there and rubbed the water out of his eyes.

He brushed his mouth against her chin and trailed his tongue to the hollow of her neck.

He scooted back against the shower wall, letting the water drizzle over him.

When he looked at her, he felt like he was drowning in her eyes. He felt his stomach tighten as he smoothed his hands over her thighs. She moaned and murmured her approval. He traced the band of her underwear with his thumb before he slipped a hand inside. He parted her slick folds with his finger and she purred. He thought he would explode. He loved to hear her satisfied groans. Kissing her deeply and possessively, he lowered himself on top of her.

Drake leaned his head against the tile as more memories rushed back to him.

Love wrapped her long legs around his waist and they linked fingers, gazing into each other's eyes. He wanted her unlike anyone else. He wanted to claim her and make her his forever.

"I want you," he whispered.

She smiled. "Have me."

He kissed her nose, then her chin. His mouth closed

*around her breast and he heard her gasp. His tongue
swirled around her nipple until she dug her nails into
his biceps. Releasing the nipple, he kissed his way
over to the other one, taking it into his mouth and giving it the same attention. Her nails scraped against his
scalp as he kissed his way down to her navel.*

Drake closed his eyes as his body reacted to the
memory. His heart pumped with excitement.

He began to enter her, and—

"Drake!"

He jumped and immediately registered the cold
water pulsing down on him. Cursing, he stood up,
pushed the shower door open, and stepped out.

The knocking continued. "Drake! Can you hear
me?"

"What?" he yelled.

"The concierge is here," Lovely told him.

Swearing, he wrapped a towel around his waist
and yanked the door open, practically pulling her into
the bathroom.

She tried to regain her balance by grabbing him.
Her hair was wet, her face flushed. Her hazelnut-
colored skin was still moist. Grabbing her waist, he
steadied her.

When their eyes met, she pulled back. "He's out in
the sitting area," she said, tugging on her robe.

"Did you ask him what he wanted?" The small
opening in the bathrobe gave him a glimpse of her
breast and he tried not to look. Really. He didn't want
to remember taking it into his mouth. He let his eyes
wander over Love's curves. If there was a contest for
best female anatomy, she'd win hands down. Her skin
was flawless; her hair was like an ebony waterfall.

And she was all natural—no weave, no acrylics, no color contacts and no silicone.

"Drake, did you hear what I said?" she asked.

"Huh?"

"I said he asked for you," she told him. "Said he had something to give you."

Adjusting his towel, he secured the knot. "Can you...?"

"Oh." She hurried out of the bathroom, bumping into the door on the way out.

He slipped his sweatpants back on hurriedly. When he came out of the bathroom, Love was sitting on the bed, shoulders slouched. Grabbing a T-shirt, he pulled it on. He wondered if she'd remembered anything. His thoughts drifted to his roaming hands...her flat, quivering stomach...the sultry moans coming from her full lips. Shaking his head, he strode past her and into the living room.

The concierge greeted him with a wide smile. "Good morning, Dr. Jackson. I trust you had a wonderful night." He shook his hand.

"What can I do for you?" Drake asked.

Love appeared in the doorway. She folded her arms across her robe and leaned against the frame.

Drake shifted his attention away from her and back to the concierge, who was eyeing Love with interest. Drake cleared his throat. "How can I help you?"

The short man coughed. "Oh, I'm sorry. I didn't mean to disturb you."

"You didn't," Drake told him.

"I just thought you might like this," he said, holding out a small box.

Drake grabbed the box and examined it. "What's this?"

The concierge laughed. "Very funny, Dr. Jackson." He patted him on his shoulder. "We rushed this up as soon as it was sized."

Opening the box, Drake gaped at the huge diamond ring. "Why did you bring me this?"

The man shifted. "You ordered it, Dr. Jackson. Last night."

His headache suddenly grew worse. "I didn't order this."

"You and the missus were in the hotel store and you purchased it."

Drake pretended he didn't hear Love's gasp or feel her body leaning up against his back as she gawked at the ring in his hand. "The missus? What the hell are you talking about? I'm not married."

"Uh, sir, you and your wife approached the front desk attendant and asked to purchase the ring from the hotel jewelry store." The man motioned to Love. "It was around three o'clock this morning. You told him you were on your way to your wedding."

"My what?" Drake bellowed, struggling to remember that part of the evening. "This has to be a mistake. I'm not married. And what kind of jewelry store is open at three o'clock in the morning?"

"W-well, you insisted," the concierge stuttered. "Your wife spotted the ring in the display case. You paid for it with your credit card and she gave us her ring size. Trust me, it was a legitimate transaction."

Advil. Better yet, Vicodin. He sat on the edge of the couch and pinched his forehead. Could this day get any worse? It wasn't enough that he had made love to his best friend and remembered only bits of it. Obviously, there was more to last night than sex.

"Are you sure, sir?" Love asked. "Maybe someone stole Drake's wallet and used his credit card to purchase this ring?"

The concierge sucked in a deep breath. "Ma'am, perhaps the problem was too many drinks?"

Drake flew to his feet, twisted the man's lapels in his fists and pulled him closer—nose to nose. "Watch your mouth. Perhaps *you* got the situation wrong." He let him go, shoving him back a bit.

After straightening his tie, the concierge smoothed a hand over his suit coat. "I'm sorry, Dr. Jackson. But you purchased the ring. I'm sure we can pull up the security cameras." He drew an envelope out of his inside pocket. "And this was sent over via courier this morning."

Drake snatched the envelope and ripped it open. Love rested a hand on his arm and he glanced at her. She was stunning, and she smelled like warm vanilla. Forcing his gaze away, he pulled the thick paper out and scanned it. Sighing, he handed it to her.

"Oh, my God!"

Drake rolled his eyes. "You said this was around three?" he asked the concierge.

He nodded. "Yes, according to Bill, the manager in charge. By the way, I wanted to come here in person to let you know that we've upgraded you to the honeymoon suite."

"This can't be happening," Love mumbled.

"Honeymoon suite?" Drake asked.

"Yes. To show our appreciation for your business."

Running his hand through his hair, Drake told him, "I don't need to switch rooms."

"We've already made the arrangements," the concierge insisted. "A bellboy will be here shortly to collect your things and transfer them to your new accommodations."

"This is Vegas." Drake crossed his arms over his chest. "People get married here all the time. Why upgrade us?"

"Well, after the amount you spent in our hotel store, it's our pleasure."

Drake didn't want to ask the question, but he had to. "How much is the ring?" he groaned.

"This is an original design, worth more than the price you paid."

"How much?" he repeated.

"We agreed on a discounted price of $15,000."

Love let out a colorful curse, then covered her mouth.

"Fifteen thousand?" Drake roared. "Are you crazy? They knew we were drinking and they still let me pay that much money for a ring?"

"Like I said, sir, you insisted," the man responded.

"Thank you," Love told the concierge. "We appreciate your hospitality. Can you leave us alone for now? We need a moment." She walked him toward the door. More like pushed him. "And we appreciate the gesture, but the honeymoon suite is not necessary."

"Certainly, Mrs. Jackson," the man said, with a wide smile. "Please let us know if you change your mind."

"We will," she assured him. "Thank you again. Have a good day."

"I will and—"

She closed the door before the man could finish his sentence.

Drake clutched the ring box in his hand. "I spent $15,000 on a ring, Love."

She squeezed his shoulder. "Drake, we'll figure this out. We'll find the receipt and try to return it."

"Good luck with that. They sold it at a discount. It was probably a final sale."

"We have to find your wallet," she said, hurrying into her suite bedroom.

He followed her. She picked a pair of discarded pants off the floor and shoved her hands into the pockets. He checked his coat and discovered his wallet was there. He opened it, leafed through the receipts and found nothing. "It's not here. I'm screwed," he said, dropping the wallet on the dresser.

She propped her hands on his shoulders. "Drake, we got married. We don't remember our wedding. We had sex, after almost thirty years of innocent friendship. Screwed is an understatement. But all is not lost, because we still have our brains. So I say we go find the—" she glanced at the wedding certificate "—Hunk O' Burning Love Wedding Chapel and try to get this thing annulled. Then we can check with the jewelry store."

Love grabbed an outfit and disappeared into the bathroom.

"Okay, Mrs. Chipper, what if this can't be fixed?"

She emerged from the bathroom a few minutes later, wearing a pair of capri pants and a tank top. "I'm not dealing with that right now. The worst has to be over."

Another knock sounded, and they heard a familiar voice from the other side say, "Lovely, open the door."

Her eyes widened. "Oh, my God."

He shook his head. "See, that's where you're wrong. It's not over—not by a long shot."

Chapter 3

"Don't answer that." Love wrapped a hand around Drake's arm. The constant knocking was getting to her, but she could handle it. "Maybe she'll go away."

"Have you met your mother?" Drake asked.

"She can't come in here." Gloria Helen Washington was the last person Love needed to see today. "She'll know what happened."

"How? We're both fully dressed." He peeled her hand off him. "Just act normal." He hurried to the door and opened it.

Gloria breezed into the room. "Lovely Grace Washington, what is your problem? What took you so long to answer the door?"

Love rolled her eyes and crossed her arms over her chest. As if naming her Lovely wasn't bad enough, her mother had added Grace to it. As soon as she was old enough, she'd insisted everyone call her Love. "What is it, Mother? You know it's early."

Love knew she hated to be called "Mother." Gloria wasn't your average stay-at-home mom. As a child, Love could be found chanting during a windstorm watch, and running around in a bright bandanna and a tie-dyed T-shirt. Yes, her mother was a hippie and damn proud of it. Even in her sixties, Gloria still had a carefree way about her. Her gray curls were wild and free, and she wore loose-fitting, flowing clothes at all times. Her mother thought the world would be a better place if everyone embraced love, hence the name.

Growing up had been pretty traumatic for the straitlaced Love. She was the only black kid in the neighborhood who wore sandals in the winter and listened to Jimi Hendrix. Instead of Ring Pops or Now & Laters, Love was forced to munch on celery sticks and snap peas. No hopscotch or Foursquare for her. Gloria thought it best that she recited poetry in the park. And Love hated poetry. Yet, even though they clashed often, Love adored her mother. And she was proud of the independent woman she'd become after the divorce. Her mother went from doting on her husband to owning one of Vegas' premier flower shops. Gloria was famous for her floral creations.

Her mother pulled her into a tight hug. "I've missed you, my baby girl. The rest of the family should arrive sometime this afternoon. Thank you for gracing us with your presence this year. You know, it's been years since you've attended. Everyone always asks about you."

The rest of her family was as colorful as her mother, which often caused a problem for the Love.

For years, the Nelson family gathered on her grandmother's birthday in March for a family reunion. Each year, the reunion alternated between several states to give each leg of the family a chance to plan it. Love had managed to avoid the last several due to school and work, but since the reunion was back in her childhood hometown, her mother had threatened to haunt her in life and death if she didn't attend.

Her mother had obsessed about this reunion for over a year, since she was the only member of the family that lived in Las Vegas. The hosting family always stayed at the hotel with everyone else, and Gloria needed Love's assistance to help make the reunion a success.

"Like I had a choice," Love grumbled, wrenching herself out of her mother's arms.

"Don't get smart." Gloria smoothed her hair back and grinned at Drake. "Hello, Drake. I'm so glad you're here." She embraced him.

"Good to see you, too, Mom," Drake said.

Love's best friend had called Gloria that for as long as she could remember. Drake and Gloria had a loving relationship and Love often found herself on the outside looking in at the two of them. They shared the same taste in food and television, preferring big steaks and fried potatoes with their zombie and sci-fi shows.

"You're looking handsome as ever, son."

"Mother," Love said, cutting in, "I know you want to talk about the reunion, but I have to make a few runs. Then I wanted to visit with friends."

Peering up the ceiling, Love let out a long sigh. She hated lying to her mother. Love was many things, but a liar wasn't one of them. She lacked the ability to make it convincing, even though she'd tried to perfect the skill growing up. Although she had made plans to visit with her friends, she had no intention of doing so now. She had business to take care of, a marriage to annul.

"Love, this is family time." Gloria picked at her daughter's hair with a frown on her face. "Why did you straighten your beautiful curls?"

Love pushed her hands away. "My hair is fine. And I promised them I'd stop by. The last time I came home to visit, I wasn't able to spend any time with my friends."

Gloria dropped her purse on a chair and scanned the room. "This is nice," she said, as if she couldn't care less what Love wanted to do. "Listen, a couple of your cousins really wanted to come but they couldn't afford a hotel. I figure they can sleep in this big ole room with you."

"No," Love said. "That's not possible. Drake is my roommate. The second bedroom is his."

"I can get my own room," Drake offered.

Love glared at him. "Mother, how about I catch the next flight back to Michigan, and they can have this room? Or better yet, I can go stay at your house."

Gloria lived in the Las Vegas suburb of Summerlin South. It was just fifteen miles from downtown. The house held many fond memories for Love and she'd love to get away and sleep in her old room for the night.

"That's not a good idea," Gloria said. "You need to stay and be in the thick of things, with me."

"It's actually okay. I figure I can spend some time in my childhood home, prepare the house for the cookout you want to have there on Sunday." Love scratched her neck and tried to ignore the skeptical look on Drake's face. He must have caught the sarcasm.

"Okay," he said, elbowing her. "I'll book a room for them. My treat."

"Thank you, Drake," Gloria gushed. "I just love you."

"So it's settled, Mother." Love picked up her mother's purse and handed it to her. "I have to finish getting ready now. I have so much to do."

"Wait, I wanted to ask you something. I'm planning a visit to Ann Arbor in a few weeks. Do you have room for your dear old mother?"

Love adored her mother. She really did. But Gloria Washington was a professional nagger. The last time her mom had stayed with her she'd rearranged everything, put all her canned goods in the recycle bin, threw away her favorite socks and insisted Love eat those nasty breakfast bars filled with millet grains.

"Uh…w-well," she stammered, "I would've said it was no problem, but I…it would be awkward."

"Why?"

That one word was enough to make Love hyperventilate. Briefly, she wondered if her mother would accept it if she answered the question with a whopping "because I said so." Or better yet, a big fat "nunya."

"Why, Lovely?" Gloria asked again. "You have a huge three-bedroom condo you're renting all by yourself. Why would it be awkward? Unless you lied to your mother about living alone?"

Love hated when her mom referred to herself in the third person. She struggled to find a suitable excuse. "I meant to tell you sooner. I don't live alone anymore."

"A roommate?"

"Kind of," Love lied. Again. She pressed a hand to her stomach, uncertain why she felt the need to tell her mother she had a roommate. *I have to throw up.* "The economy is rough. I figured it would help."

Gloria's eyes flitted back and forth between Love and Drake. Finally, she placed a hand on her hip. "When did you start lying to your mother, Lovely?"

Damn. Caught already? "Why do you say that?"

"You hate living with anyone. You wouldn't even let Drake move in."

Love shifted her attention to Drake, who was watching her with a smirk on his face. Although he was her best friend, she had turned him down when he'd asked to stay with her while he found a place. Instead, she'd suggested that he book a suite at the Marriott closest to the University of Michigan Hospital, where they were both residents. He was pissed, and didn't hesitate to tell her. Love had assured him it was the best thing for their friendship. She adored him, but there was no way she could live with him. Drake was your typical smelly, messy and loud man. Not to mention a man-whore.

"Mother," Love said. "I didn't want to tell you this, but…" She stalled, running a list of possible roommates in her mind. "Drake *is* my roommate."

He gaped at her.

The room was silent for a few minutes as both of them absorbed this news.

"Drake?" Gloria asked. "That's impossible."

"It's the truth. But I can't really talk about this now. I told you I have plans."

"No, I want an explanation. If Drake is your roommate, you'll never find a man who wants to marry you."

Drake snorted and Love smacked his shoulder.

"When did this end up being about marriage?" she asked her mother. "Wait…don't answer that." It seemed as though these days, every conversation between them contained a reference to the *M* word. "Please, Mother. I promise we'll spend lots of time together. Later. I'll answer all of your questions then." She hugged her. "Love you."

Gloria stomped to the door. "Okay, Lovely. Take care of your business. But we are going to talk about this. And since Drake is your roommate, he won't care if I stay there for a few days. Right, Drake?"

He shrugged. "Sure," he said drily.

Love opened the door to let her out, only to find the concierge on the other side, preparing to knock.

"Mrs. J—"

"Hi!" Love said. "Did you need something?"

"I forgot to give you the receipt from the jewelry store."

She snatched it from him. "Okay, thanks. Bye."

"Who is that?" Gloria asked, shoving her out of the way.

"Mom," Drake interrupted, pulling her from the door. "It's just the concierge. I purchased something and he was bringing the receipt. Thanks again." He pushed the door closed, but the concierge stopped it with his toe.

"One more thing, Dr. Jackson. Just a reminder—this is a final sale."

Love sighed.

Drake muttered a curse. "Fine."

"Thanks for your business, Dr. Jackson. And congratulations again." He turned to walk away and Love let out a sigh of relief—until he glanced back at them over his shoulder. "Please let us know if you choose to take us up on the offer of using the honeymoon suite."

"Honeymoon suite?" Gloria repeated.

"Yes," the man said, tugging at the lapels of his suit as he lifted his chin. "We here at the Bellagio love to cater to our important guests. Nothing more important than a wedding."

"Whose wedding?"

"Do something," Love mouthed to Drake.

"Mom, how about we go get breakfast?" he said, nudging Gloria away from the concierge. "I'm starved."

"Wait a minute," she exclaimed, digging in her heels. "Who got married?"

"Why, *they* did," the chubby man replied with a toothy grin. "They visited our jewelry store to purchase the ring."

"Oh, my God." Love leaned her forehead against the wall.

Gloria turned to them. Tears welled in her eyes, and she fainted.

Chapter 4

Drake watched as Gloria's eyes rolled back in her head.

"Mother!" Love called. But it was too late.

Gloria fell like a heavy tree and nearly slipped through Drake's arms, but he was able to catch her. Grunting, he carried her to the couch. "Get my bag, Love," he ordered.

She sprinted into the bedroom, came back with his medical bag and dropped it on the floor next to him.

The concierge had followed them into the room. Drake glared at him. "You can go now. I'll handle this."

"Maybe I should call an ambulance?" he suggested.

"No, she should be fine. Like I said, I've got this. I'll call if we need anything."

The concierge glanced at Love. When she nodded, he left the room without another word.

Drake assessed Gloria, checking her airway and pulse, while Love propped her legs up on a pillow. Her pulse was strong. "Mom, can you hear me?"

Gloria moaned softly. "Lovely…"

Love knelt in front of her and picked up her hand. "Mom, I'm here."

Gloria's eyes fluttered open. Drake let out a quick sigh of relief. Gloria was many things, but mostly she was as much *his* mother as she was Love's. Gloria had been the only motherly figure he'd had, since he hadn't known his real mother. She had stepped in and filled the gap. Drake had never gotten along with his stepmother, and he'd been grateful that he'd had someone in his life who had supported him through everything.

"Mom, are you okay?" Love's voice pulled him back to the present. "You fainted. Have you been taking your medication? Your insulin? Did you eat this morning?"

Gloria was a diabetic. Over the last few years, she'd had several complications as a result of her illness that had required Love to fly out to Vegas and take care of her. The most recent hospital stay was only a few months ago, and Gloria's doctors had suggested amputation due to lack of blood flow to her legs and feet.

Love had recently told him that she'd been trying to convince her mother to get a second opinion at University of Michigan Hospital, but her mother had declined. Drake knew it bothered Love that her mother lived so far away and seemed to be getting worse.

Drake poured a glass of water and handed it to Gloria, who took a sip.

"I'll be okay, baby." The older woman struggled to sit up. Eventually, she simply leaned on her elbows. "Baby, please tell me…"

Love peered at Drake. "Mom, don't think about anything right now. You need to lie back. No sudden movements."

Gloria shook her head and finally sat upright. "I told you I'll be okay." She smacked Love's hand away when she tried to keep her from rising to her feet. "You need to tell me what's going on. And, Drake, if you don't tell me the truth, I'm calling your father."

The threat of his dad knowing anything that was going on in his personal life was enough to give Drake pause. Gloria had used that threat often on him, growing up. It was the only thing he'd ever responded to. Simply put, he couldn't stand his dad. Life with him had been one disappointment after another. The safe haven that Love and her family had provided had saved him.

Dr. Lawrence Jackson, plastic surgeon extraordinaire, had always been too busy working and having affairs with random women to even care what Drake did in his personal life. What the man cared about was that Drake was surgical resident, studying to take over his own thriving practice. Except Drake never intended to become his father. In fact, he'd worked tirelessly to distance himself from the man who drove him insane with his demands and unrealistic expectations. Instead of plastic surgery, he'd chosen cardiothoracic surgery as his focus, much to his father's chagrin.

The only thing he'd loved about living at home was his siblings—two brothers, one sister and his uncle El, who was like a brother.

The last thing Drake wanted was his father involved in the mess he'd gotten himself into. No doubt there would be a long lecture that would end in him cursing his dad out and Love urging him to apologize out of respect.

"Mother, please." Love stood and straightened her clothes. "It's not what you think. That man doesn't know what he's talking about."

Drake cleared his throat. "Mom, you fainted. You need to relax a bit."

"I'll relax when both of you explain to me how you came to Vegas, got married and didn't tell me."

Gloria's sudden high-pitched screech caught him off guard, and he jumped.

"Why are you screaming?" Love covered her ears.

"Because!" She stood finally, pulled them both into a tight hug, and kissed Drake's check. "This is so exciting. Why didn't you tell me? You should have let me know."

There was something about her tone that made him a little suspicious.

Love pulled out of the group hug. "Mom, you don't understand. It —"

Gloria gasped. "We can have a small reception. Yeah. We can do it in June. That will give me enough time." She sat back down on the sofa, then rifled through her purse and pulled out her phone. "June 10 is perfect. Oh my, I have to get out of here. I have to tell your father, Love."

Threatening to tell *his* father was one thing, but

there was no way *Love's* father could know what had happened. He was, after all, Drake's boss.

Drake nudged Love. "Do something."

She stood there, her mouth hanging open.

"Give us a minute, Mom." Drake pulled Love into her bedroom and slammed the door. "Love, say something to your mother before she tells the whole free world," he demanded through clenched teeth. "She threatened to tell my father. And did you just hear that she's going to tell *your* father? He'll hop the next flight, then he'll kick my ass before he fires me."

Love tugged at his shirt. "We have to do something."

Drake muttered a curse. "Ya think? We need a game plan. First, you need to get your mother."

"Now she's *my* mother. *You* need to handle this, since you're her favorite."

He threw his arms in the air. "Please, Love. The man came in here with the receipt for the ring, and told her that we're married because our drunk asses actually did that last night. The sooner you get that through your head, the sooner we'll be able to figure out what we're going to do to fix this."

She placed her palm over his mouth. "Shh, you're getting too loud. She'll hear you."

He counted to ten and took a long, deep breath. "Do you understand why I'm a little concerned right now?" he asked, when she removed her hand.

"Of course I do. But we don't know the circumstances," Love argued. "We don't even know if this certificate is legal. And if we really are married, we won't be after today."

Drake grabbed her shoulders. "That's all fine and

good, but before we figure that out, we need to get your mother under control. And that means coming up with an explanation for the concierge's visit. She's not going to buy one of your crazy, nonsensical lies."

Gloria's loud laugh carried through the door.

He pointed in that direction and frowned. "Is she on the phone?"

Love bolted out of the bedroom and snatched her mother's cell out of her hand. Ending the call with a quick "Sorry, gotta go," she handed the device to Drake. "Mom, who were you talking to?"

"Your aunt. I was just getting ready to tell her about your happy news. She's going to be so excited."

Drake wrapped an arm around Gloria and steered her over to the couch. "Mom, I understand it was a lot to take in at once. But you've got this all wrong."

Her smile faded. "Care to explain?"

He glanced at Gloria. "Yes, you deserve an explanation."

"Aren't you happy that you married my daughter?" Gloria asked, concern evident in her brown eyes.

Drake was torn. The question was a double-edged sword, and any answer he'd give would be bad, in her opinion. He'd always been truthful with Gloria, but he couldn't be now. If he told her the truth—which wasn't an option—he'd be admitting that he'd married her daughter in a drunken state, in a cheesy Las Vegas wedding chapel, and he wasn't happy about it. If he said yes, the response would send her on a rocket to heaven and it would take a miracle to bring her down. There had to be a middle ground. He glanced up at Love, who was staring at the floor. *No help.*

A knock sounded and drew their attention to the

door. Drake hoped it wasn't that damn concierge returning to make matters worse. He stood and followed Love across the room.

She glared at him before she pulled the door open. In front of them, on his knees, with a ring in hand was Love's ex-boyfriend.

Oh, my God!

Love swallowed at the sight of the jerk who'd broken her heart, and the gorgeous ring in his hand.

"Love, you're beautiful." Derrick flashed a dimpled smile. "I couldn't let another day go by without telling you how I feel. I love you. I want to marry you. I want us to have forever."

Love was speechless. She'd dreamed of such a proposal from Derrick Harper when they were together—over a year ago. He was successful, cultured and handsome. He was everything she'd thought she wanted. The life he could offer her was appealing on some level. But the pain that he'd left in his wake still stung. The horrible breakup had devastated her, and she'd gone out of her way to avoid him. In fact, she hadn't seen him since. And now he was proposing? She couldn't believe this was happening.

"What the hell are you doing here?" Drake asked incredulously.

Derrick rose to his feet. The smile he'd been sporting a few seconds earlier turned into a sneer. "Drake. I guess I shouldn't be surprised that you're here."

"Answer the question." Drake's voice was a low growl, and Love knew that this confrontation could turn physical. Drake had never cared for Derrick. The way Derrick broke up with her—with a text—had made Drake's disdain grow by leaps and bounds.

"Derrick?" Gloria stepped between Drake and Love. "You're here."

Love frowned at her. It wasn't a question, and there was no hint of surprise in her mother's tone.

"How did you know I was here?" Love asked him, knowing the answer already.

"You didn't tell her I was coming?" Derrick asked Gloria.

She averted her gaze as a blush crept up her neck to her ears. She pushed a strand of her gray hair behind her ears. "I didn't. But you can leave."

Derrick narrowed his eyes. "What? We talked about this. I flew all the way here."

"Mother, how could you?" Love felt the sting of tears in her eyes.

"I didn't. Your father called and asked for the details of the family reunion. He told me that Derrick wanted to win you back, because he realized he made a mistake letting you go. I'm sorry, Lovely. I should have told you, but I thought I was helping you."

Love couldn't stop the snort that escaped. "Help? You encouraged a man who broke my heart to come to my family reunion and propose? Mother, do you realize that he broke up with me with a text message, after he cheated on me with his colleague for months? That means I wasn't worth more than a few characters."

She felt Drake's hand on her shoulder. The soft squeeze that came next soothed her frayed nerves, and she shot him a grateful glance out of the corner of her eye.

"I've got this," he whispered in her ear. "Harper,

you're out of order. For you to show up, after a year, and expect her to fall into your arms and accept that whack proposal, you must be crazy. It's obvious to me that you don't think much of Love."

"How is this your problem?" Derrick asked, his dark eyes icy.

"Love is my problem. When you don't respect her, I have a problem with it. You've already hurt her enough. I'm not going to stand here and let you try to insert yourself back into her life so you can do it again."

"Drake." Love squeezed his arm. "I'm okay."

He looked down at her, his eyes soft. He shook his head slightly before turning a hard glare back to Derrick. "Get out. Go home. Don't call her again."

Derrick snickered. "Why don't you let Love talk?"

Drake stepped closer to him, nose to nose. "Don't let the fact that I'm a surgical resident make you think that you won't see these hands."

Gloria spoke up. "Derrick, you need to go. It's too late, anyway. Drake and Lovely are—"

"Mother, stay of this," Love snapped. The way her mom had reacted to the news of the marriage hadn't been a shock. Gloria had always shipped a potential Love and Drake union, and she was itching to tell anyone that the two of them were married. Love couldn't let that happen. So far, they had managed to not outright admit it to her, but they hadn't fully denied it, either.

Shaking her head, she turned her attention back to the two men in front of her ready to go to blows any minute. "Derrick, you need to leave. You're not welcome in my life anymore."

"I don't believe you." He held up the ring. "You know we belong together. It just took me longer to realize it. I was stupid, full of myself. Then I realized that you were everything to me. I want to marry you."

"I can't do this," Love said, pulling Drake back out of the doorway. "I'm done." Without another word, she slammed the door in Derrick's face.

Drake barked out a laugh. "That was good. I'm proud of you."

"Lovely, I'm sorry." Gloria pulled her into a hug. "I'm so sorry. I should have never listened to your father. Why didn't you just tell Derrick that you and Drake were together?"

Sighing, Love backed away from her mother's embrace. "Mother, I need a minute. I'm upset and I need to talk to Drake. Alone."

Gloria's shoulders fell. "Fine. I'll go." She gathered her purse and headed toward the door. "I'll see you at the dinner tonight, right?"

Love turned away from her hopeful stare, and nodded. "I'll be there. And, Mom, please don't say a word to anyone about what the concierge said." She didn't give Gloria a chance to answer, but simply walked into the bedroom and closed the door.

Chapter 5

Love sat on her bed and stared at her painted red toenails against the plush beige hotel carpet. It had been several hours since her mother had left. She and Drake had gone to the Hunk O' Burning Love Wedding Chapel, only to find that it was closed due to a "family emergency."

Drake had then sped to the Clark County Courthouse, only to find that it was closed until the following Tuesday due to an unpaid furlough day. Needless to say, Drake was pissed and had cursed during the whole ride back to the hotel.

She heard the door open and looked up to find him standing in the entranceway. "I'm hungry," she said.

"I ordered you something through room service."

She chuckled. Despite how infuriating Drake could

be at times, he still knew her like the back of his hand. "Thanks," she mumbled.

"We need to discuss this." He sat on a chair on the other side of the room, far away from the bed.

"Not if you're going to yell."

"I won't."

Love scooted back and leaned against the headboard. "Let's talk, then."

"We're going to have to carve out some time to fly back and get this taken care of. In the meantime, we just act like nothing has changed. We keep avoiding your mother's questions, and go back to Michigan like nothing happened. I'm not sure we would be granted an annulment, because of the..." He scratched the back of his head.

"Sex?" she interjected.

"Right." He shifted in his seat. "Once it's done, we can tell your mother that it was a big misunderstanding and we're not married."

Love stared at the ceiling, unable to say anything at that point. She wondered if he was going to actually address the fact that they'd had sex, since he'd had a hard time even saying the word.

"I'll take care of the court fees," Drake continued. "I did some research on the process."

As he explained the process, Love didn't let on that she'd done her own research on the way to the chapel earlier. They didn't even have to appear for a hearing in certain cases, and they definitely had grounds for an annulment because they'd been intoxicated at the time of the marriage.

Love picked at the comforter. "We can split the

fees. I think we should hire an attorney to take care of everything else."

He nodded. There was a soft knock on the door. Drake disappeared and came back minutes later with the room service tray. They quietly ate lunch. It was the first time they didn't say anything to each other. They'd always been able to talk, to laugh at and with each other. Now, they were in a sea of awkwardness, and she couldn't take it anymore.

"Drake, don't you think we need to talk about the fact that we had sex? I don't want this to be a thing between us, one that we can't get past. I need you in my life."

He shrugged. "What can I say? We had sex. After all these years, one night of tequila and we did it. I guess I just don't know what to say about it."

Love turned, to find him picking at his food. "I remember."

Drake gave her a sideways glance. "Me, too."

Over the course of the day, she had been able to recall the details of last night, all the way up to the rushed wedding at the gaudy chapel. They had spent the evening visiting casinos on the Strip and drinking. She wasn't sure when it happened, when something had changed between them. She just knew it did, and all of a sudden, they couldn't deny the attraction, couldn't stop touching and kissing each other.

"It was my idea to get married." While they'd watched the fountain display at the Bellagio, Love and Drake had kissed. Things had heated up quickly, and Love recalled how she'd announced that she wasn't having sex again until she was married. That's when

Drake had proposed by singing "Suitelady (The Proposal Jam)" by Maxwell. The rest was history.

"We were pretty twisted," he said softly. "I'm not even sure how I let it happen."

Love wasn't sure why she felt deflated at his comment, but it stung.

"I wanted you," he admitted. "In a way I never thought possible. It was a need I couldn't shake away, or convince myself it didn't exist."

She peered up at him, caught his gaze, before he averted it.

"I remember that part," he added. "I'm not sure how I can forget it. It certainly can't be undone." He stood and joined her on the bed. "But you're more important to me than anybody in my life. I'm willing to try."

A lone tear escaped down her cheek and he swiped it away with his thumb. "I hate myself for doing this, for depriving you of your first wedding. I know how much you wanted that. And you deserve it, with someone who is going to love you and treat you well."

Love closed her eyes. The dig at Derrick was clear. Yet she couldn't help but feel sad that Drake blamed himself. "It's not your fault. I wanted it, too. You were sweet, gentle and tender. And I appreciate that."

He squeezed her hand. "We can do this, right?"

Love didn't know if they could or not. She only knew that she would work hard to make sure it wouldn't destroy their friendship. Instead of answering him, she pulled him into a hug. One of his hands swept up her back and rested on the nape of her neck. Prior to yesterday, that would have been a normal

Drake thing to do. But in the aftermath of the night before, it was doing all kinds of things to her body.

Her instinct was to pull away, but she couldn't let herself do it. Not only would pulling away shine a bright light on the way they had changed their relationship with their actions, but she had to admit it felt good to be in his arms. Drake was the only man who made her feel safe. Her father didn't even have that title. It was only Drake. Regardless of what they did or didn't do with each other, she needed him like she needed her next breath.

"Yes, we can do this," she answered finally, holding on to him even tighter.

After an uneventful family dinner, Drake and Love had settled in for cocktails and conversation with her mother and her aunt. The dance was in full swing, and all around them the Nelson clan was mingling and catching up.

Love and Drake had both let out a sigh of relief earlier that Gloria had kept her mouth shut during the organized program, especially when the MC asked if anyone had any announcements. Now, as they sat at a high top table with her mother and her aunt, Love watched Drake interact with various members of her family. They absolutely loved him, and he managed to charm most of the women in the room with his deep dimples, smooth dark skin and beautiful white teeth. He was dressed in a navy suit with an azure-blue shirt that fit him to perfection, and she noted the way random women had responded to him all night.

"You want to go play?" he whispered in her ear.

She choked on the water that she'd just taken a sip of. "What?"

He flashed a knowing grin. "The slots?"

"Oh." She wiped her mouth with a cocktail napkin. "Nah, not right now."

Love enjoyed the slots. But if heading to the casino floor was anything like the walk into the banquet hall that evening, she'd pass. Drake was a gentleman, so it was second nature for him to keep his hand against the small of her back as they walked. Since her navy blue, knee-length dress was cut low in the back, every so often the tips of his fingers would brush against her bare skin, stirring her nerve endings. It also didn't help that he smelled like spice mixed with a burst of citrus.

Absently, she wondered if it would be this way forever, now that she'd been with him. As much as she wanted to act like it never happened, separating the Drake that held her hair up while she hurled in the toilet in college from the Drake that made love to her at her favorite hotel on the Strip was proving to be harder than she thought.

"Drink?" he whispered.

She could smell the cognac on his breath, and fought against an urge to lean in closer to his warmth. Exhaling, she told him no. She'd stick with water. "You don't have to hang around if you don't want to."

"I'm fine." He finished off his drink. "Your mother did a good job with the dinner."

"She did." Love grinned at him over her shoulder.

He beckoned to the waitress and ordered another drink. Then he turned to Love. "You look nice tonight."

Smiling, she tapped a finger on the table. "You don't have to say that."

"I know," he said simply, with a wicked grin. "I hope they know we didn't plan to be color coordinated."

Unable to help herself, she burst out in a fit of laughter. "I know! I can't believe that happened."

When his distinctive laugh followed, she pressed a hand to her quivering stomach as relief washed over her. They could still relax and make each other laugh.

The clink of glasses drew their attention toward her mother and the microphone she was holding in her hand.

Oh, no.

"Can I have your attention, please?" Gloria began.

The chatter in the room dimmed to a dull roar. Drake dug his fingers into Love's knee.

"I am beside myself with glee because my daughter made it to this reunion. It's been a while and I'm so happy she's here."

Love stood up abruptly, hitting the table with her knee. *Oh, God.* Rubbing her knee, she called out, "Mom, what are you doing?"

"I want to say to Drake that I love you like a son," Gloria continued, as if Love hadn't spoken. "And I'm so happy that you're a permanent part of my family now. I want everyone to congratulate my daughter and her new husband, Drake, on their marriage."

A round of claps and multiple cheers erupted. Love's throat closed up as people swarmed her. Leaning against the table, she searched for Drake in the crowd. She took a few cleansing breaths as her stomach churned. Her throat became dry, and she reached for her glass of water. It was empty. Then Drake was there, behind her, leading her away.

The roar of the crowd disappeared, replaced by the bells of the slot machines, then silence. She struggled to breathe, grasping at her throat frantically.

"Sit here," he said, gently setting her on a hard ledge.

She heard the sound of running water and, seconds later, felt a warm cloth against the back of her neck.

"Love, breathe," he whispered, as his hand closed around hers. "It's okay." He pressed the cloth against her forehead and rubbed her back.

A few seconds later, she felt her airways open up. "Drake."

He knelt in front of her, holding a glass of water in his hands. "Drink this." He held the cool glass up to her mouth, and she gulped it down.

Wiping her mouth, she shot him a smile. "Thanks."

"You have to be careful, Love. It's been a long time since you've had one."

Love had been known to have panic attacks in the past. And more often than not, Drake had been there to pick up the pieces. That was why he—as annoying as he could be—was the most important person in her life. The first time it had happened to her, back in high school, she'd thought she was having a heart attack. Over the years, she had been able to manage them. Drake was right. She hadn't had an attack in a long time, but after the events of the day, she wasn't surprised.

"Did she just do that?" she finally managed to ask.

He nodded. "Yes, she did."

"She's going to come find us." Love imagined her mother searching frantically for them. She glanced at the small room, and realized she was sitting on a toilet. Frowning, she searched his gaze. "You brought me into a bathroom?"

Drake shrugged and blew out a short breath. "I didn't have many choices. You needed to get out of there. And I asked your mother to give us some time."

Love leaned forward, rested her head on his shoulder. "What are we going to do? This is a nightmare."

He leaned his chin on her head and wrapped his arms around her in a tight hug. "We'll be okay. She didn't tell a lie. We did get married, in a moment of obvious lack of judgment. So we have to deal with the consequences."

She pulled away, searched his eyes. There was no panic in them. He was calm, as usual. "How can you not be freaking out about this? What happens when my dad finds out?"

He rolled his eyes and looked away from her. Standing, he took the washcloth and tossed it in a bin. "If your dad finds out, we'll deal with it. In the meantime, we have to tell your mother the truth."

"What truth? That we got married on a whim because we had too many shots and wanted to get our freak on? I don't know if I can do that here. She's so happy, so proud. I'm sure she thought I was vying for spinsterhood, and this just gave her life. Besides, the whole family is here."

And with her mother's progressing diabetes and her recent diagnosis of peripheral artery disease, Love thought that she needed some happiness.

Drake sighed. "So, we wait until after the reunion is over."

"Maybe we should just wait until we can get an annulment. Or a divorce," she added under her breath.

"The fact that my father called my mother to get the deets on the reunion for Derrick makes me think they talk a lot more than I thought. She would definitely tell my dad we got married. He won't be happy with you. He'll kill you."

"What do you suggest we do? We're not going to stay married, Love."

Love looked down at the tile, focused on the grout between the gray, beige and ivory colored squares. "Let's make it through this weekend. When we get home, we'll hire an attorney to take care of it. We can tell everyone that we made a mistake and decided to fix it before our friendship suffered for it. This way, my dad won't be too upset, because he'll think I did this willingly, and he won't take it out on you or your career."

Drake didn't answer for what seemed like an eternity. Love rubbed her thumbnail over one of the sequins on her dress.

"Okay," he said finally. "We'll wait until we're home and divorced to break the news to your mother."

Love stood, then stepped closer to Drake. She tilted her head to meet his gaze. "Drake, I need you to promise me that we won't let this ruin us."

His eyes softened, and he pinched her chin as he had so many times before. "Love, we won't. You're my best friend and nothing is going to change that."

A tear fell from her eyes, and he smirked.

"You're such a baby," he said, grabbing a tissue and holding it out to her. "Get cleaned up, so we can go play the part of a loving couple for a few minutes."

Love went to the mirror and grimaced at her raccoon eyes. "How about we just go back up to the room and let them think we snuck away because we're in newlywed mode? I look like a crazy woman." She eyed him in the mirror. "Hmm?"

"You're beautiful."

He turned her to him and his finger trailed down her nose before he hooked a hand behind her neck and pulled her closer. When his lips touched hers, it felt like a dream. The kiss wasn't passionate, but achingly sweet. It was soft, warm. Just what she needed in that moment.

He pulled away and grinned. "Whatever you want." He brushed his thumb back and forth over her earlobe. "You go on up, and I'll find your mother and tell her that we're turning in. I'll also ask her to not tell anyone else, because we want to make our own announcement back in Michigan."

Love let out a nervous laugh and tried to pretend Drake hadn't just kissed her knees wobbly. "Let's hope she listens."

He wrapped an arm around her and led her out of the bathroom. "I'm praying she will."

Chapter 6

The warmth of Las Vegas had been replaced with a Michigan snowstorm. In March. Ann Arbor was the sixth largest city in "The Mitten," as some people called the state. It was home to the Ann Arbor Art Fair, "The Big House," the annual Hash Bash, Zingerman's Delicatessen and the University of Michigan.

Love had dreamed of attending "U of M" as a child. Maize and Blue was in her soul, running through her veins. Except she hadn't expected Ann Arbor to be so cold, wet and humid at times. She had grown up in Las Vegas, after all.

Still, in her time there, she'd come to love the quaint college town, with its parks, many shops and diverse population. And the food...yum. *I'm so greedy.*

Love walked through the University of Michigan Health System, now known as Michigan Medicine, greeting several people in the halls. There was a flurry of activity as always, with individuals from all walks of life milling around. A musician played on a grand piano in the lobby area and patients readied themselves for appointments. As a medical resident, focused on Obstetrics and Gynecology, Love been assigned to all the many hospitals within the system. Her favorite, of course, was the Von Voigtlander Women's Hospital, attached to the C. S. Mott Children's Hospital. Considered one of the nation's leading medical institutions, Michigan Medicine was on the cutting edge in many specialties, and Love was happy to be a part of it.

The elevator doors opened on floor five and Love rushed out, nearly slipping on the linoleum. Gripping the edge of a nearby counter, she stood still for a minute, taking a few deep breaths. It had been a day since she'd awkwardly said goodbye to her *husband*. They'd successfully finished the reunion weekend without ending up in bed with each other again. Which was a good thing. Well, that's what she kept telling herself, anyway.

Except for that kiss. One kiss, and she'd felt like her world had titled on its axis. She'd been going back and forth about bringing it up. Sure, they'd had sex and got married, but that night of the reunion dinner he'd kissed her deliberately, while sober. Then he'd acted like nothing extraordinary had happened. She hated him.

They'd agreed to talk before she headed into work this morning, but she'd avoided his many calls. After a night of Drake-filled dreams, talking to the man was the last thing she needed.

"Hello, Dr. Jackson."

Love stopped in her tracks and turned when she heard his name spoken, and Drake's low-voiced response. He was grinning, like the flirt he was. And the stupid nurse who'd greeted him was eating it up. There was nothing about the encounter that was abnormal. Drake was well-known and well-liked by the staff, especially the women they worked with. Last week, the overly friendly nurse wouldn't have bothered her, but this week that damn nurse was talking to her husband.

Closing her eyes tight, Love willed the jealousy away.

"How was your trip?" Nurse Annoying asked Drake.

"Good," he answered. "How was your weekend?"

Love rolled her eyes when the nurse flipped her hair and giggled like a teenage girl with a crush before relaying the details of her weekend clubbing and drinking with her friends.

"I was wondering if you liked Thai food?" the nurse purred, reaching out to fix Drake's collar. "There's a restaurant that just opened up around the corner. I happen to be free for lunch, if you want to join me."

Tramp.

Drake and the woman turned to face her, and Love realized that she'd spoken out loud.

"Really?" the nurse snapped.

"I'm sorry," Love mumbled. "That was inappropriate."

"I called you this morning," Drake said to her, an arch in his brow. A signature trait that seemed even more endearing today. "We were supposed to talk."

Love looked at the nurse, then at Drake. "I know." She fidgeted, squeezing her purse between her palms. "I was busy."

"Too busy to discuss Vegas?"

Love motioned to the nurse, who was listening intently. "Can we talk about Vegas later?"

"What happened in Vegas?" the nosy woman asked, folding her arms across her chest. "Wait, you went to Vegas with Dr. Jackson?"

"Actually, Drake went to Vegas with me. And shouldn't you be administering some medication this morning?"

"Rita, I need to take care of something right now," Drake told the nurse.

She actually had the nerve to pout. "What about lunch?"

Love couldn't help it; she opened her mouth and it came out. "Drake, don't you think you should run along and get that infection checked out before it spreads?" She flinched when he pinched her.

"She's lying," Drake assured the nurse. Then, after a scalding glare in Love's direction, he added, "About lunch... I don't think it's a good idea. I don't mix work and pleasure. Sorry."

"Oh, I—I didn't mean a date," she stammered. "I was just asking as a friend."

"Give me a break," Love mumbled.

The nurse backed away and stumbled over a wheelchair. "But I understand, Dr. Jackson. I'll see you around."

Love covered her smile with her hand, but Drake chuckled out loud. And even though he'd blatantly laughed at her and boldly rebuffed her advances, Love was sure the other woman wouldn't hesitate to let him take her to bed. That's just how women were around the handsome, eligible Dr. Drake Jackson.

Love slung her bag over her shoulder and started for the residents' lounge, with Drake on her heels.

His hand around her arm stopped her. "Love, wait."

"Drake, I have to get started. I want to talk to Dr. Hastings about my patient." Since finding out in Vegas about the woman's death, Love had been rolling her entire history with Mrs. Rodriguez in her mind. Her father had once told her to never get too personal with her patients, but she couldn't help it. "I have many questions."

Drake let her go, and ran a hand through his hair. "Love, we can't deal with this if you keep avoiding me. We have to put on a united front here at the hospital."

"Why? No one knows anything."

They'd managed to get her mother to promise not to share the news with anyone else, so Love felt secure in the fact that no one in Michigan would know unless they told them, and they'd decided not to tell anyone.

"Yes, I know. But there is the pesky detail of hiring an attorney to handle the annulment."

She forgot. Sighing, she scratched her ear. "Okay, you're right. Come over tonight and we'll talk about it."

Drake hesitated, tapped his foot against the floor. Nodding, he pulled his phone out of his jacket. "I'll be over after five. I have to go."

He walked away without another word. Love watched him round the corner toward the patient elevators. Nibbling on her finger, she sighed and entered the residents' lounge.

"Hey, you," Lana called, approaching her. "What are you doing here? I thought you weren't coming back for a few days?"

She peered up at Dr. Lana White and smiled. "Hey. No, I was always supposed to be back today."

It was always good to see Lana. Her cousin was like a breath of fresh air in her life. Love had been a lonely kid. Her mother's diabetes had prevented her from having more children, so Lana had been a stand-in sister. She was popular and intelligent and had taught Love all about boys and science.

Lana dropped a file on the table and plopped down in a chair. "Girl, it's been boring as hell without you."

Love set her bag in her locker and quickly dressed in her scrubs. "I wasn't gone that long."

"Did I tell you that my life and my stomach depend on you to be around?" She laughed, rubbing her flat belly.

Lana was a mess in the kitchen, so Love had spent many a night cooking for her. "You're so greedy."

"Hey, there is no shame in my game."

The two shared another laugh. Lana could eat anyone under the table, but looking at her, one would never know that. She was a natural beauty, with perfect skin the color of rich toffee. Her cousin was slender and toned at five feet nine inches tall. For a long time, Love had envied Lana's long legs, silky hair and confident stride. It had taken years for her to feel comfortable in her own petite frame, especially when around her gorgeous cousin. For all intents and purposes, Lana was the only girlfriend she had. It was a bonus that she was also a close relation.

"I saw Drake zoom past me," Lana said. "He barely said two words to me."

Love froze. "Oh? He's probably going to see El." She pulled a bag of veggies from her roomy purse, closed her locker, and plopped down next to Lana.

"El, huh?"

Love didn't miss the interest in her voice. For years, she'd hoped that El and Lana would connect as more than friends. Unfortunately, El hadn't been interested in dating since he'd broken up with his ex-girlfriend Avery. Poor Lana had been crushing on him for quite some time.

They sat in silence for a moment, before Lana stood. She opened the fridge and pulled out a bottle of water. "I'm hungry. I'm gonna head to the cafeteria. Care to join?" She took a long gulp of water.

"I'm married," Love blurted.

Water sprayed out of Lana's mouth onto the floor and the wall. "Damn," she exclaimed, grabbing a napkin and wiping her face. Then she placed a hand on her hips. "What did you just say?"

Love hurried to wipe up the spilled water before meeting her gaze. "You heard me."

Lana wrapped an arm around Love's shoulder and guided her over to a couch on the other side of the room. They both sat. "I heard you, but I don't understand. The Love I know went to Vegas single, and now you're standing in front of me telling me that you're married. Who did you marry?"

Love swallowed, hugging herself. "You have to promise not to tell anybody."

Lana shrugged. "Who am I going to tell?"

"Promise me."

"I won't say anything."

Love tucked her feet under her bottom and relaxed a bit. "After you called and told me about Mrs. Rodriguez, I was beside myself with grief."

"I know. I had to convince you not to come back, remember?"

"Drake took me out to distract me."

Lana bit her lip. "So, what's different about that? Drake is always there to distract you."

"I know, right? But this time we woke up the next morning in bed together."

The blank look on Lana's face told Love that her cousin still wasn't following. "So what? I don't know why, but you two have been known to share a bed. Often. I'll never understand how that worked between you, but hey. To each her own. Not many women can sleep in bed with a man as fine as Drake and not be tempted to…explore. And vice versa." Lana took another swig from her bottle of water.

Oh, boy.

Lana rambled on, obviously ignoring what had to be a sick look on Love's face. Or maybe she just felt sick? "You're a good catch, too," her cousin continued. "Any man would want to be with you. You're gorgeous." She took another swig of her water.

"Naked." Love jerked back when water sprayed on her face. "Damn, Lana. Can't you control your spit reflex?"

"Oh, no. I'm so sorry." Lana grabbed a handful of tissues from the table and dabbed Love's face. "You can't spring something like that on me."

Snatching the tissue away from her startled cousin, Love muttered a curse. "Anyway, long story short, I couldn't remember what happened the night before. But there was evidence of sexual activity on the bed."

Lana frowned. "Evidence? Why do you have to sound like an old episode of *Law & Order*? So mechanical. What kind of... Oh! And you don't remember having sex with Drake?"

"Keep up, Lana. I didn't remember when I woke up next to him naked. I remember now."

"You had sex with Drake," she whispered.

"Why are you whispering? There's no one else in here. Yes, we had sex."

"Was it good?"

Love gaped at her amused cousin. "Stay focused."

"Okay. I'm focused. I'm putting on my doctor's face. Detached and listening Lana here. Answer the question."

Lana placed a hand over her mouth and let out a squeal of...delight? Then she cleared her throat and straightened in her seat. "Okay, you have my undivided attention."

Love hesitated before she continued the story. "Then the concierge comes up to the room with a ring."

"A ring?"

"Yes." Love took a deep breath. "I married Drake in Vegas."

Lana's mouth fell open. "Get out of here."

"Believe me, I wish I wasn't telling the truth."

"You and Drake got busy *and* married in the same night? After all these years of pure, platonic friendship, you just chucked all the unspoken rules out the window and did it?"

Love hung her head.

"This is too juicy not to share."

Love shot her a death glare. "If you say one word, I will kick your ass up and down this hospital."

Lana's hands went up in surrender. "Okay, okay. I won't say anything."

Love pointed at her cousin. "I swear, Lana. Don't play with me."

Lana squeezed Love's knee. "My lips are sealed. Calm down. But you have to admit, this is good tea. Blogworthy. You, Ms. Queen of Control, had sex and got married, while drunk, to your best friend." She barked out a gleeful laugh. "No one would believe me if I announced it on the loudspeaker during rounds."

Lana was right. No one would believe it. Love had to admit that, if she hadn't been there, she wouldn't have ever thought she was capable of being so reckless. She filled her cousin in on the plans for an annulment. "And there's one more thing."

"There's more?"

"My mother found out."

"Gloria knows?" Lana asked with wide eyes. "Oh, God. You must be mortified."

It was no secret that her mother wanted Drake and Love together. She'd just given up on that hope after years spent denying they were anything more than friends.

"And she announced it in the middle of the family reunion."

"Oh, Jesus. Does Uncle Leon know?"

"No, thank God. I convinced Mom not to say anything to my father. But you know her. She is giddy with excitement. And when she's excited, she's crazy."

Though Lana was her cousin on her father's side of the family, she knew Gloria well. She still spent her summer vacations in Las Vegas with Love, even after Love's parents divorced.

"This just gets better," Lana mused aloud. "How do you feel?"

"How do you think? Drake can barely say the word *sex* in front of me, and I can't look him in the eyes. It's a nightmare."

"I think you two should definitely talk about it. It's going to be a huge elephant in the room. Not to mention awkward for everyone else around you. And if you don't want Uncle Leon to find out about it, you best air this before it starts to affect your friendship."

It was a truth that Love had been worried about since she'd landed at the Detroit Metro Airport the night before. Drake seemed normal enough, but their situation was anything but.

"How is Drake acting?" Lana asked, concern in her dark brown eyes.

"He's Drake. Calm under pressure. He doesn't look at me like we had sex."

That fact alone made Love feel totally inadequate. Drake had told her he wanted her, but he never said he'd enjoyed their lovemaking. Just that he remembered it. She knew him. Had seen him when he was into a woman, heard him talk to El about women that he found entrancing and unforgettable. Her worst fear, which really shouldn't even be a fear, was that she was a bland blip on his sex radar. The thought of being one of those forgettable women he never talked about made her feel sick. Especially since everything about that night was memorable for her.

What was more frightening? That he didn't enjoy it, or that she'd enjoyed it too much?

"Love, it's going to be all right," Lana said, as if she sensed the turmoil inside her. "You and Drake will work it out. You have to. Life wouldn't be the same if you and Drake weren't…you and Drake."

Love smiled and leaned into Lana, who hugged her. "Thank you, cousin. Love you."

Love's cell phone buzzed in her pocket. Hoping it was Drake, she grimaced at the sight of her father's number. She unlocked the phone and read the text: In my office in fifteen minutes.

Something told her there was another wrench in her best-laid plan.

Chapter 7

"El, we need to talk." Drake barged into El's office, closing the door behind him.

Dr. Elwood Jackson sighed and told his secretary, "Give us a minute."

Drake hadn't even realized there was someone else there, but he couldn't care. He needed to talk to his uncle. "You need an hour," he said.

"Block my calendar off for an hour," El told the shy woman as she exited in a hurry. When the door closed, El tapped on the desk. "This better be good. You know I'm busy."

Drake took a seat on the couch in the office. It was the one El used when counseling his patients, and he had half a mind to stretch out and start the conversation with "I'm going crazy." Instead he simply said,

"You're a shrink, but you're also the closest thing to an older brother that I have."

El was his father's youngest brother, and technically his uncle. But he was only five years older than Drake, who liked to call him his uncle-brother. El had told him to drop the "uncle" from the title years ago, but Drake used it sometimes to get on his nerves.

"What's going on, Drake?" he asked, leaning back in his chair. "You're acting out of the ordinary."

Drake slapped a dollar bill on the desk. "Now what I'm about to tell you is restricted under doctor/patient confidentiality."

El smirked. "Really? You're paying me a dollar? What the hell is happening?"

Drake leaned forward, his hands flat on the desk. "This is serious, El. What I'm about to tell you is a game changer. And I need your ear and your advice."

El rubbed his chin and nodded. "I'm listening."

Drake managed to get the sex and marriage thing out in one sentence. But it annoyed him that five minutes later El was still laughing. While his uncle-brother snickered at his expense, Drake grew more and more frustrated.

Tapping his fingers against the desk, he finally yelled, "Give me my damn dollar back. You're no help."

El coughed in an effort to stifle his laughter. "I'm sorry. I'm just… I can't believe we're having this conversation."

"Last I checked, me talking and you laughing is not a conversation."

"You're right." El cleared his throat. "Let me get

this straight. You had drunken sex with your best friend, married her, and now…"

"That's it. We're still married."

"Why this trip to Vegas? Why now?"

"How the hell should I know? I'm not sure what happened to turn this into what it is. One minute we're hanging out on the Strip and the next we're married."

"What did Love do?"'s

"Freaked out. Especially when her mother announced it to the entire family reunion," he mumbled under his breath.

"What?" El blared. "When did Gloria find out?"

"She happened to be in the room when the damn concierge dropped by with the happy news and the receipt for the $15,000 ring I bought her."

"Fifteen thousand!"

"I can't talk about that. Man, if I wasn't there, I wouldn't believe it. What the hell was I thinking?"

"I'm wondering the same thing."

"Thanks."

"This is not like you, which leads me to believe that a part of you wants to be with Love in some capacity. Do you think that's why you did this?"

Drake frowned. "El, what the hell? You know me. You know Love."

"You're not answering the question. *Impulsive* is not a word I associate with you or Love. Neither are *sex* and *marriage* after years of friendship. I'm just wondering if there wasn't a part of you that's always wanted to be with Love on that level."

Drake thought about that for a minute. Love was beautiful, hands down. And not just physically, but her beauty radiated from within. For years he'd watched men try to get close to her, drawn to those special inner qualities. She was an exceptional cook, she loved sports and she loved him—flaws and all. That meant something to Drake, made him want to deserve someone like her. But he wasn't the type to settle down. He wanted the high life and a high-rise in the city, women in every town and no expectations. Love wanted the small-town life, a husband who came home at a reasonable hour every night, kids, and family vacations. And Drake wanted that for her.

He was wise enough, though, to know that Love had ruined it for any woman he'd meet in the future. He'd always compared any prospective woman to her, and the other woman always lost. But that wasn't something he'd ever shared with anyone else. It was his secret and he'd keep it that way.

"No," he grumbled. "A relationship with Love will not work. We want different things in life. She deserves better than me."

"Ah," El said.

Sighing, Drake shifted in his seat. He hated that "ah" El pulled out during serious conversations. It meant that he surmised something about Drake that Drake would undoubtedly resent.

"In a perfect world, would Love be the one you want? I mean, you both have some weird codependency on each other. She's your girl without being your girl. I know you've been friends for a long time, but it's very telling that the minute your inhibitions were lowered, you slept with her and committed to each other officially. Have you asked yourself why?"

Drake stood abruptly, paced the floor. "Stop asking me questions like that."

"Well, you did pay me."

"To buy your silence, not to prescribe me medicine and be my psychotherapist."

El chuckled. "You do realize that one dollar doesn't even buy you a minute of my time under normal circumstances."

And this was the downside of having a shrink for an uncle-brother. El always tried to find the hidden emotions in everything. Drake was tempted to inquire if El had asked himself all these whack questions. Maybe his uncle-brother wouldn't be afraid to move on from Avery.

"To answer your question," Drake said, "we don't live in a perfect world. Because if we did, I wouldn't be going through this right now."

"Is it possible that you have feelings for Love that go beyond friendship?"

It was a trick question. There was no right answer. If he said yes it would affirm El's suspicions of hidden emotions. If he said no it wouldn't make any sense, since they'd spent the night together rolling around in bed naked.

"She's my best friend."

"Like a sister?"

Drake snorted as he paced. "Hell no." He had a little sister, and knew what sister feelings were. His friendship with Love had never been like that. For starters, he didn't admire his little sister's legs or her cleavage. "But we've known each other since we were toddlers."

He and Love had never crossed a line with each other. Drake had never given her kisses behind the chalkboard in kindergarten, made forts in the backyard so they could play house. No Hide-and-Go-Get-It in the wooded trails behind the school. There was no picking on her boyfriends because he was jealous.

"This is going to sound like a strange question, but did you enjoy it?" El asked.

Drake whirled around. "What?"

"Did you enjoy being with her?"

Drake clenched his fists and stretched his neck. "I—I…" he sputtered. "It was sex. I enjoy sex."

"Once again, you're not answering the question. Did you enjoy being with Love on that level? It's a simple yes or no answer."

"Of course." Drake scowled at El. "Like I said, it was sex."

"Was there anything about the experience that was different than your other sexual relationships?"

"Yes!" Drake blared. "It was different because it was her!" The sheer exhaustion he felt after that admission made him sit back down on the couch. Hard. Arms on his knees, he leaned forward. "I can't stop thinking about it. Once I remembered the details, it's been running through my mind on a loop."

Every kiss, every touch of her lips to his…it still burned there. It wasn't simply making love. They made fire together. Hot, scorching fire that had seared his brain, stayed with him. Seeing her that morning in her snow boots and puffer coat, looking into her expressive brown eyes, had made him want a repeat.

"I don't know what to do with this," Drake admitted. "Things are different. I'm trying to keep it the same but I still feel her, smell her. She's not in the 'can't go there' box I put her in all those years ago.

I've gone there, and I can't flip a switch and pretend I didn't."

El coughed. "Okay, so let me ask you…what are you going to do about it?"

What can I do? Any move he made ran the risk of destroying everything, and he'd promised he wouldn't let what happened ruin them. "Nothing. The sooner we can end this marriage, the better."

The answer wasn't one he liked. He'd have to put some distance between them if their friendship had any chance of surviving. She'd already been hurt enough by Derrick. Drake couldn't hurt her.

His phone buzzed with a message, breaking him from his thoughts. When he saw who it was from, he groaned loudly.

"Who is it?" El asked.

"Her dad." Drake glanced at the text again: My office now. "I have go. I'll call you later.

Walking to Dr. Leon Washington's office was like walking the plank. It wasn't that Drake hated him. It was quite the opposite. Drake's own father was a lousy one, and Dr. Leon had filled in a lot of gaps for him as a child.

Drake's parents had never married. His mother was one in a long line of mistresses that only served one purpose in life for his father. When Drake was born, his father took custody of him, and he could count on one hand the number of times he'd actually seen his mother. He'd met her once after his kindergarten graduation. The second time was an unplanned incident at the mall when he was a teenager. He hadn't even recognized her when he saw her but she had walked up to him and gave him a hug and a kiss before she disappeared from his life for good. He'd found out she died a few years later.

His father's wife never showed him love. He figured it was because he was the constant reminder of the man's infidelity. There was the kind nanny and the housekeeper. Then there was Gloria. His father and Love's dad were colleagues and the two families spent a lot of time together. Dr. Leon had taught Drake how to drive, how to change a tire. He'd helped him study for the MCAT and wrote letters of recommendation to medical school.

Somehow, Drake knew that marrying his daughter was a different story. The elder man, his boss, had made it clear that Love was off-limits. Yes, Dr. Leon was firmly in Derrick's camp, as evidenced by the fact that he'd sent the fool to Vegas to woo Love back.

Drake rounded the corner toward Dr. Leon's office and slowed when he spotted Love pacing outside the door.

"Love?" he asked, approaching her. "What are you doing here?"

"What are *you* doing here?" she asked.

"Your dad texted me and told me to come."

"Me, too."

"Great," he mumbled.

She looked up at him, tears swimming in her eyes. "Do you think he knows? What do I say?"

The relationship between Love and her father was strained, had been since Leon divorced Gloria, married his mistress and moved to Michigan. It was partly because of his high expectations of his daughter, but mostly because of the divorce and everything that had happened afterward. Her parents had had a contemptuous relationship, but the one thing they'd never argued about was her. Her father had never fought for her. He was completely okay with summer and holiday visits, which infuriated Love.

She'd once shared with Drake that she knew her father was overbearing, but a part of her always wanted to please him, even though he didn't deserve her loyalty. She even went so far as to date a man handpicked by her father. Derrick. The asshole who'd cheated on her for months.

Drake ran his finger down her cheek, and she leaned into it. There was nothing he wouldn't do to stop her tears. Even lie, cheat or steal. "Don't cry," he whispered. "It could be a total coincidence that he asked to see us both. Don't worry, until we have something to worry about. Besides, he won't take his anger out on you. I'll be the one doing cholecystectomies for the foreseeable future."

She giggled. "Stop making me laugh."

"You know I'm right."

"Probably. He won't even give you those gallbladder surgeries. You'll be lucky if he lets you scrub in on an appendectomy."

"My bet? I'll be stuck in the ER intubating patients all day or on central line placement."

She nodded. "Ready?"

He knocked on the door. When he heard Dr. Leon beckon them to come in, he opened it. He expected to see Love's father with his head buried in a chart, or writing on the whiteboard in his office. Instead, Drake froze when he saw Derrick Harper sitting comfortably in front of the desk.

Dr. Leon stepped forward and met his gaze, the

frown on his face telling Drake this wasn't a friendly visit. "Well, well," he said. "If it isn't the newlyweds."

"Daddy?" Love said, her voice shaking as her gaze moved between Derrick and her father. "What's going on?"

"You tell me," Dr. Leon said, gesturing for them to take a seat.

Love held on to Drake's hand and squeezed it tightly. Her father was a formidable doctor, in and out of the operating room, but what distinguished him from other surgeons was his willingness to teach. He'd mentored students across the country. Right now, though, he didn't look so amenable.

Dr. Leon ran a hand over the stubble on his chin and let out a heavy grunt. "Since you're not talking, how about I start?" He pointed at Derrick, who sat with a smug look on his face. Drake wanted to kick his ass. For the life of him, he didn't understand what Love had seen in the man. He was a jerk, plain and simple. And Drake knew jerks, because he was an ass on a good day. "Imagine my surprise when Derrick told me what happened in Vegas when he arrived to propose. Not only did he walk into you and Drake sharing a hotel room, but he overheard your mother announcing to a roomful of people that you're married."

Drake glared at Derrick.

"What?" Love said. "You were there?"

"I went to the dinner to talk to you," Derrick said. "I left when your mother announced the marriage."

"And you couldn't wait to come back and tell my father?"

"Never mind that," Dr. Leon said. "Why? Are you pregnant?"

Love shook her head. "No. We'd never… I mean, it's not like that."

"Drake?" Dr. Leon said. "Care to say something? I believe you owe me an explanation."

"I do. But I'm not talking about this with him in the room." Drake couldn't believe he'd basically told his boss to kick someone out of his office. "This is between me, you and Love. Not Derrick."

Leon glared at him. "Listen, you married my daughter without so much as a call for permission. After everything I've done for you."

Love gasped. "Daddy, don't—"

Drake glanced at her out of the corner of his eye. "Love, let me handle this." He met her father's hard gaze with one of his own. "With all due respect, sir, this isn't about you. It's about me and Love. He doesn't belong in this room."

"Who do you think you're talking to?" Derrick asked incredulously.

Drake stood. "Did I stutter? I meant what I said."

"Well, luckily, this isn't your office." Derrick sneered at him.

Drake looked at Dr. Leon. "I've known you for a long time. You're like a father to me, especially since my dad couldn't be bothered. I think I deserve a chance to talk to you without an audience."

"If you have something to say, say it," Dr. Leon challenged.

Drake squeezed Love's hand when she gasped. "Dr. Leon, the fact that we're even having this discussion stings. I thought you knew that I would never intentionally hurt Love."

"I don't think you'd intentionally hurt her," Dr. Leon responded, his voice flat.

Drake couldn't figure out why the older man, his mentor, was choosing to treat him as if he was no better than a random guy on the street. He knew Dr. Leon wouldn't be happy, but this was another level of disdain that he'd never expected. Love's father was stern, not overly affectionate, but he'd never been a jerk. It rankled Drake, made him want to confront the older man, his job be damned.

"I know my daughter, and there is more to this story."

It was laughable that Dr. Leon was standing in front of him, telling him that he knew Love. "I understand that you think you know your daughter, but when are you going to admit that I know her just as well—probably better? I know what she wants out of life, and I will do my best to make sure she realizes her dreams. As I'm sure she'll do for me. There is nothing I wouldn't do for her." It was the truth, and Love knew it. That's why he could be found watching chick flicks on a Saturday afternoon, or visiting every single new art exhibit in the area, or snoring through off-Broadway plays. "And I don't really care what anyone else has to say about it, because I've got her."

Leon stared at them, long and hard.

"I'd love to continue this conversation," Drake told him. "But I need you to ask that fool to leave."

Dr. Leon held his ground. "Derrick is family."

The comment stung, especially since Drake respected Leon, modeled his professional career after him.

"Family?" Love said. "Really, Daddy? Drake is family, legally now. I know you're upset, but he *is* my husband. Derrick is not, and never will be because he broke my heart."

"Lovely Grace Washington!" He bit out the words like she disgusted him. "I'm your father and you will respect me."

"When are you going to respect *me*, Daddy? This man cheated on me and broke up with me via a text message. But you don't seem to give a damn. Maybe because you did the same thing to Mom."

"Lovely!" Dr. Leon shouted.

"No. I can't believe you're even entertaining Derrick after what he's done."

"This is the first I'm hearing of it," her dad argued. "You told me things just didn't work out between you and Derrick."

"Well, now you know. Do something about it."

Drake wasn't surprised Love had his back. She always did, willing to go into battle for him at any time. "Calm down," he whispered against her ear as he massaged her shoulders. "This isn't helping."

Love jerked out of his hold. "No. I'm sick of being calm. Daddy, since you love Derrick so much, you marry him."

Then she stormed out of the office, slamming the door behind her. Turning on his heels, he went after her.

"Drake?" Dr. Leon called to him.

He stopped at the door, but didn't turn around.

"We're not done yet."

"We are today," Drake said. "I need to go see about my wife."

Chapter 8

Love burst into the lounge area carrying her patient charts and her dreaded, ringing cell phone. It had been ringing nonstop since she'd stormed out of her father's office that afternoon. Frustrated, she never even looked to see who was calling. She was pretty sure that Drake, her mother and Lana were among the many callers. But she didn't care. She wanted to be alone.

In five minutes, she'd be safely outside in the frigid air. Anything was better than the hospital at that moment. She'd finish her chart notes at home. Luckily, she didn't have appointments that day. Love pulled her bag out of the locker and dropped her phone and files inside.

She didn't stop stuffing her bag when she heard

the door open and close behind her. Instinctively, she knew it was Drake. "Go away."

"Love, we have to talk."

She groaned when a traitorous tear escaped. "No, we don't. I'm done talking today. I'm going home. Alone."

"You can't just run away."

She turned around, glared at him. "Why not? I need some distance between us right now."

Because she couldn't tell him that the way he was willing to go up against her father, his boss, for her made her swoon inside. She slung her bag over her shoulder and headed toward the door.

"Wait," he called.

When he caught up to her, she turned to him. "Just let me go, Drake. I have to go."

"Why are you flipping out on me? What did I do?"

"You didn't do anything, Drake. I'm irritated. And you know I hate to feel this way."

"We're in this together."

She peered up at the ceiling. Last week, her life had been boring but she loved it. Today, her life was anything but boring and she was unraveling at a rapid pace. "I can't do this right now."

"Stop being emotional. I need you to talk to me, like you're Love and I'm Drake."

"Drake, please. I'm tired, and you're damn right. I'm emotional." As she talked, a different type of energy took over. Anger. "We are married. When I envisioned holy matrimony, I pictured a white dress, fresh flowers, soft music, my friends and family surrounding me, and my father walking me down the aisle. I wanted to *remember* the most important vows I'll ever make and look back with fondness at my wedding pictures on my silver anniversary."

It seemed odd to others, but after Derrick broke up with her, she'd wanted to abstain from sex until she found the man she was going to marry. She'd promised herself that the next time she made love to anyone, it would be her husband. Her goal was to replace bad sex memories with good ones, lasting ones.

"Not only did that not happen, my father basically said he didn't give a damn that the guy he wants for me is the asshole of the century. My mother is running around planning wedding receptions." She ticked off the reasons on her fingers. "And my best friend, my husband, is acting like we're going to just get over the fact that we had sex and got married on a whim. As much as I'd like to believe that this will be a story we share with our real spouses someday in a fit of laughter, it's unrealistic."

"Love—"

"No, Drake. There is nothing you can say to make this better right now. Please back off. I want to be alone."

"Okay," he said simply.

That one word infuriated her even more. Pivoting on her heels, she stalked off and slammed the door behind her.

Twenty minutes later, she was in her home, climbing into bed. Closing her eyes, she took in the fresh linen smell. Her emotions were playing mean tricks on her and she couldn't take it.

She had no idea what she was going to do. Drake had been her best friend forever. There was little they didn't know about each other. But his presence was making it worse, with his kind eyes, and the way he cared about her. It was distracting, and she needed to get a grip.

Her father had hurt her. She'd purposefully withheld the real reason she'd broken up with Derrick. Instead, she'd chosen to downplay it as two people who'd grown apart and couldn't take the weight of a long-distance relationship.

In reality, long distance suited her just fine. It was the infidelity that had made her blood boil. And the lies had sealed his fate. But instead of taking it like a man, he'd chosen to end it first with a short, harsh text message.

To have her father simply shrug it off like it didn't matter devastated her. It shouldn't have surprised her, but it did.

Her parents' divorce had been absolutely the worst period of her life. Drake had spent countless nights holding her as she cried herself to sleep. Her father had moved to Michigan during her freshman year of high school, the same day her boyfriend had dumped her for not putting out. Drake had stolen a fifth of tequila from his father's stash and shown up at her house to keep her company.

Smiling, she recalled her first foray into the world of tequila. They'd spent hours talking about nothing and taking shots, before she'd hurled on his brand-new sneakers. There would be many more nights of them being there for each other. When Drake received word that his mother had died, she'd been the only one who could console him.

The sound of her phone buzzing drew her out of her memories. She glanced at it and read Drake's text:

I know you're pissed. I'll give you a few hours, then I'm coming over for dinner. Make something good. I'll bring dessert.

She couldn't help the small laugh it elicited. He always could cheer her up. Then she typed in her response: I'm not cooking. But I want a decadent and expensive dessert.

Love turned her phone off and rolled over on her side. A nap was exactly what she needed. As she lay there, her eyes feeling heavy, she prayed sleep would come sooner rather than later. Yawning, she burrowed into the down pillow.

"I, Lovely, take you, Drake, to be my lawfully wedded husband."

"I like the sound of that," Drake murmured against her lips. Nipping at her ear, he whispered, "I, Drake, take you, Lovely, to have and to hold from this day forth. Forever."

His mouth brushed against hers before kissing her fully. The searing kiss that followed curled her toes, it was so good. His lips were soft, but firm. And she was lost in him.

"Did we really just do this?" she asked, peering into his hooded eyes.

"Yes." He swept his thumb under her chin, down her neck.

Her eyes fluttered closed as he kissed her eyelids, her nose, then her mouth. "Drake, did we make a mistake?"

"If we did, it's the best mistake I ever made."

He kissed her again, pulling her flush against him.

*Without warning, he picked her up and carried her
out of the chapel.*

Love's eyes popped open, and she sat upright as
their wedding night replayed in her dream. Again.
Every detail filled her mind—from the touches, the
kisses, the— *Shit.*

He'd kissed her with a sweet tenderness she'd never
felt from him before, and she'd wanted him like no
other man before him. It was a perfect wedding kiss,
one that could and should go down in the record
books. He'd at least given her that. As butterflies tickled her stomach, she relived the moment they'd come
together, him inside her, filling her completely. A soft
moan escaped from her parted lips at the memory. It
was everything. He'd made it everything.

Squeezing her eyes—and her legs—closed, she
screamed into her pillow. How the hell was she supposed to look at him and not think about it?

A little while later, Love shuffled into the kitchen.
Opening the fridge, she pulled out a casserole pan,
humming to herself when she looked down at the de-
lectable vegetable lasagna she'd made the night before.
She'd been so wired from thinking, she'd decided to
put that energy to good use and cook.

Her phone rang and she looked down at her mother's
face staring back at her. *Not going to answer that. Not
now.* The last person she needed to speak with was
her giddy mom, Gloria. Most conversations with her
ended up being about Love's lack of companionship
or her mother's lack of grandkids. But that was before
the eventful reunion. Now that she'd gone and married Drake, she was sure the conversation would turn
to wedding receptions and the six grandkids Gloria

couldn't wait to have. This event was bound to be a spectacle.

Despite her mother's weird ways, she'd made a name for herself as an event planner for many years before retiring to open a flower shop. Love admired her for not letting the divorce send her to the bottle or catapult her into a sinking depression. Gloria Washington had made great strides to become a formidable businesswoman. She'd started out with a few small jobs creating floral displays for her neighborhood church. One Sunday, an executive at the Bellagio Hotel in Vegas had visited the church for a function. The visitor had been so impressed by the display, she'd insisted on meeting Gloria. That meeting had turned into a job at the hotel in the Sales and Catering Department. Gloria's career grew from there, and she eventually went out on her own and opened her own shop.

Even now, no matter how she was feeling, her mom managed to get out of bed every morning and make it to work. Love couldn't be more proud.

Love checked her voice mail and text messages just in case it was an emergency. No messages, so it must not be important. *I love you, Mom. But I still don't want to talk to you.*

Cutting a hefty piece of lasagna, Love set it on a plate and put it in the microwave. While it warmed, she went to the wine rack and pulled a bottle of pinot noir from her reserves. Once she'd poured a nice glass for herself, she swirled the liquid around and took in the fruity, yet earthy, aroma. Love took a sip and let it rest in her mouth a moment before swallowing. Perfect.

The ding of the microwave signaled it was time to eat and she hurried over to retrieve her dinner plate. She heard the front door open and close, but stayed put. She knew it was Drake. He was the only one who had a key.

Her phone rang again, and she was tempted to answer if only to stop the constant calls. Out of the corner of her eye, she saw Drake stroll into the kitchen and slide a box onto the countertop. She didn't have to look inside to know what it was. The box was from her favorite bakery. Distracted, she almost didn't see the hands reaching for her plate of lasagna.

Love smacked the back of one. "Don't you dare. Get your own piece."

"Damn. Okay."

"I knew I was asking for it when I gave you a key. You're always letting yourself in and helping yourself to my food. Maybe you should leave a twenty on the counter for groceries."

"Ha. You're funny." He pulled his wallet from his back pocket and slapped a crisp twenty-dollar bill on the counter. "You know I don't eat homemade meals unless you cook for me."

Love ignored the cash and the man in front of her, and finished her glass of wine. She burped. "Get that dirty money off my counter." She cut another piece and put it in the microwave.

Once again, her phone chimed. "Is that your mom?" Drake asked.

"Why?"

"She called me and asked where you were and why you weren't answering her calls."

Great. "Did you tell her I was asleep?"

"I did."

She pulled his lasagna out of the microwave when it was done and set it in front him. He'd refilled her glass of wine and poured one for himself. They settled in for a quiet meal.

"So, I called the chapel today," Drake told her. "Everything is legit."

Love knew that. Her dreams proved that much. They'd gotten married in a cheesy, gold trimmed chapel by a minister in an Elvis costume for heaven's sake. It was too odd to not be true.

After a few minutes, Love said, "Did you know you're the third man I've had sex with?" Drake choked on his food, covering his mouth with his napkin. She waited until he finished chewing before she spoke again. "I realized that we've never been the type of friends to talk about sex—especially my sex life."

"Maybe it's because sex should be kept between the two people having it?"

She tilted her head, assessing him. Drake was her best friend for a reason. Sure, he was loud, annoying, and he could be a jerk some days. But he was sincere, sweet and loyal every day. She smirked. "Still, we've shared so much with each other and it's never come up. Weird, huh?"

For some reason, she couldn't stop staring at him, letting her eyes wander over the clean lines of his face. He was focused on everything but her, yet she found herself entranced by the mere strength of him—his strong hands, the tiny scar under his right eyebrow, the way his dark rinse jeans hugged his thighs, the tattoo on his arm that poked out from beneath his short-sleeved shirt. He was a beautiful man. She'd never really appreciated it before, but it seemed to be all she could think of in that moment.

"You're staring," he muttered, pushing his food around his plate.

"Sorry." She finished her second glass of wine and moved to the sink. As she rinsed the dishes, she heard him stand up and walk over to her. Pausing momentarily to breathe, she glanced at him out of the corner of her eye as he leaned his hip against the sink.

"Love, I'm sorry."

She swallowed. "Why?"

"I can't help but feel like I took advantage of you that night."

"Is that what's been bothering you?"

He nodded, crossing his arms over his muscular chest.

"We were both drunk, Drake. It's not an excuse, though, because we both know better. I make it a point to tell the women I see every day to watch their alcohol intake. But things happen. If I had to get drunk and throw my inhibitions out the window, I'm glad it was with you." Their gazes met. After swallowing hard once again, she said, "I mean, it's good that I had sex with you and not some random guy in a bar." *Shut up, Love.* Except she couldn't stop talking. "I'm just saying…well, I trust you more than anybody." *Just stop talking.* "And it wasn't like it was bad sex. It was good."

He picked up her hand and entwined his fingers with hers. "It was," he agreed, his voice low and husky. His thumb traced the length of hers, and her nerves stirred. "But don't you wonder why we chose that night to…"

"Have sex?"

He nodded. "We've been friends for almost thirty years. It's not like we haven't been drunk together before. Why this trip? Why now?"

"Does it have to mean something deep?"

"Shouldn't it?" He squeezed, and her gaze dropped to their joined hands. "You're a beautiful person, not the type of woman that any man—including me—should take to bed without it meaning something."

"Do you love me?"

He gaped at her and she couldn't help but laugh.

"Drake, it's not a trick question. I'm not asking if you're in love with me. Do you love me?"

"Of course I love you. You already know that. You're the most important person in my life."

"Then it means something. We can't dwell on it, though, so let's move forward."

Drake arched a brow. "And ignore that it happened?"

"Not exactly. I don't think we could ignore it if we tried."

The room descended into silence. He stood there, his eyes locked on hers, his hands holding hers. He inched closer to her.

"Love?"

At that point, she wasn't sure why she'd even started the conversation. It was bad enough that just being near him was doing all kinds of things to her body. "Yes?" she said, her voice coming out more whispery than she'd intended.

His thumb swept over her palm. "I know what you're trying to do, but it's not that simple."

Oh, God. He smells so good. His cologne washed

over her and she couldn't help but lean closer to get another whiff. Today he smelled like black pepper, leather and wood.

"I don't think it's going to be so easy to move on from this," he added.

She looked at his fingers as they drew tiny circles over her wrist and up her arm. Her heart beat in her ears as a warmth spread from her belly to her toes. He was talking, but she had no idea what he was saying. She was too entranced with his mouth, the feel of his breath on her skin. Her eyes wandered down his neck to the top button of his shirt.

Stop picturing him naked, Love.

"But you're right," he said.

Confused, she frowned and peered up at him. "Huh?"

He chuckled, and she couldn't help but smile. Touching her face, then her neck, she let out an airy giggle. *Breathe, Love. Focus.*

Drake was quiet now, studying her when she looked into his brown eyes again. And he was closer. It was almost like he could read her mind.

Oh hell, why do I want him to kiss me?

Then he did. His lips met hers in a soft kiss, one that seemed to steal her breath.

Wait, Love. The warning in her head was clear. She pushed him away. "Drake, what did you just do?"

He rubbed his chin, a frown on his face. "Uh, I kissed you."

"Yeah, you did. Why did you do that?"

"Because you wanted me to."

His answer was so matter-of-fact that she backed up a step. How the hell did he know that? "You can't just keep kissing me like that. You did it in Vegas, too. Just kissed me for no reason."

"You were upset, and I wanted you to feel better."

"So you kissed me?"

He sighed, rubbed his forehead. "I don't know. It just felt like the right thing to do at the time."

"And today?"

"I don't know," he repeated.

Love's curiosity got the best of her and she asked, "And how do you know I wanted you to kiss me?"

He shrugged, shoving his hands into his pockets. "I can't describe it. I can always tell when a woman wants me to kiss her."

"So you just do it?"

"Of course not."

"In this case you did."

"It's you. I kissed you because *you* wanted me to."

She opened her mouth to respond, but the words didn't come. His question to her earlier roared in the back of her mind. *But don't you wonder why we chose that night…?* It had to mean something that they'd had sex, married each other.

"Why?" she whispered.

"You tell me."

She sucked in a deep breath. "Maybe…"

"You want me to kiss you again, don't you?"

Love paused, shocked at his question. Not because he was being his confident, cocky self, but because he was right. She did want him to kiss her again. She wanted it more than she wanted her next breath.

"Yes," she admitted with a sigh.

She trembled as he stepped into her, pulling her to him for another kiss. His mouth moved over hers with short, languid movements. His tongue swept into her mouth and tangled with hers, drawing a low moan from her throat. His hands roamed over her back, over her butt. She felt a buzz between them, and then the heat of his nearness was replaced by a chill.

When her eyes opened, he was staring at his phone.

"Love, I have to take this. It's the hospital."

He stepped out of the room before she could formulate a response.

What had just happened? He ran off to answer his phone in the middle of a kiss, one that had curled her toes and made the hairs on her arms rise.

Her eyes darted around the kitchen until they lit on the white box on the counter and she hurried over to it. Opening it, she moaned at the sight of the deep-fried beignets. Picking up two, she stuffed both in her mouth, all the while thinking that eating beignets was not the only thing she wanted to do with her mouth.

Chapter 9

Drake leaned against a wall in Love's living room. He'd been off the phone for five minutes, but still wasn't able to go back to her in the kitchen. Because he'd kissed her. Twice. And he'd wanted to go in for thirds and more, but his phone had been his saving grace.

It wasn't anybody important, just another resident with a question on one of the patients he'd doctored that day. But it was a welcomed interruption because things were on the verge of going way left.

Drake leaned against the couch. El's words rang in his ears. His uncle-brother had surmised that sex with love had to mean something. And he was right.

He'd spent the last several nights turning every moment over in his mind, trying to find the difference. There was no clarity, no epiphany that would explain how they could go from being best friends to married within the span of twelve hours.

They'd slept in many a bed together. He'd seen her in her underwear more than a few times, had knocked back shots several nights, and still…no sex. Nothing. Now, he couldn't stop imagining it. He remembered how she'd looked beneath him, how her bare skin had felt beneath his hands.

He was tempted to leave right then and there, but he wouldn't do that to her. Groaning, Drake walked over to the wet bar on the other side of the living room and poured a healthy glass of cognac.

If he went back into the kitchen, looked at her standing there in those cute little shorts, with that damn bun in her hair, he was liable to kiss her again— or more. Everything had changed. She'd told him they needed to move past it, but could they? He doubted it, since he couldn't stop wanting her.

Yet even as he warred with himself over his next steps, he knew he couldn't run from it. With other women, if things got too hot, he'd walk away. Simple and painless. Love wasn't other women, and walking away wasn't an option. She was his closest friend, the best woman he knew, and now she was his wife.

Drake finished the contents of his glass in one gulp and walked into the kitchen. Love was standing at the island, her head down. Had he hurt her by walking away in the middle of that kiss? It wasn't his greatest moment, but that phone call had offered a reprieve, given him a chance to think before he made another impulsive decision.

"Love, I'm sorry."

The fact that she didn't respond was odd. If he'd

pissed her off, she'd lash out. If he'd hurt her, she'd cry. But her lack of response was not like her. He stepped closer, caught a glimpse of the open box in front of her.

"Love?"

Finally, he reached her and turned her around to face him. His friend, his wife, was standing before him covered in confectioner's sugar. Her cheeks were stuffed with beignets and the box was…empty?

"You ate all of the beignets? I bought half a dozen."

A burst of powdered sugar flew into his face when she opened her mouth to speak. "I'm sorry," she mumbled almost incoherently.

He picked up a napkin and wiped his face. "I can't believe it." Her lips and chin were white with powder. He poked one of her cheeks, and another puff of sugar flew out. "You're going to pay for that in the morning, ya know?"

She nodded, chewing rapidly. He poured her a glass of wine and pushed it toward her. Once she'd successfully swallowed the beignets, she gulped down the entire glassful.

"Don't laugh."

He covered his mouth. "I'm not laughing. I'm shocked."

"I couldn't resist." She grabbed a towel and scrubbed her mouth with it until her lips were red.

He gripped her wrist. "Stop."

"I'm so embarrassed." She tucked a stand of loose hair behind her ear. "I couldn't stop eating them."

"You have some…" Reaching out, he wiped sugar from the side of her mouth.

She touched where his finger had been. "I must look a mess."

"Not even a little bit."

Her eyes softened, propelling him forward until they were almost touching. He framed her face with his palms, brushed her cheeks with his thumbs. Her sharp intake of breath spurred him on. Leaning forward, he nuzzled her nose with his.

"Drake," she whispered.

The smell of sugar and dough on her breath mixed with the exotic scent of her perfume made him ache with need. Soon, he couldn't see the room around him or hear the sound of the ice maker dropping a round of cubes into the freezer. Everything simply faded away and Love was the only thing he was aware of.

"Are you afraid of what you're feeling?" he asked her.

She swallowed visibly and nodded.

"But you don't want to deny it?"

Love's answer didn't come in words. That didn't matter, though. He was fluent in her body language, and he'd heard her response loud and clear. She wanted him, too.

He skimmed her jawline with his fingertips, watched her eyelids flutter shut. "Talk to me, baby." He laid a hand on her chest, felt her heart beat fast beneath his palm.

Opening her mouth, she said, "Drake, I—"

Unable to stop himself, he leaned in and licked left-over sugar from her chin. Her lips parted more and he took full advantage, pulling her into a deep kiss. Her body was flush against his, her softness melding into his hardness as if they were meant to be like this with each other. She moaned low, raked her hands through his hair, digging her fingernails into his scalp.

He wanted to explore every inch of her skin, see her in the throes of passion, immerse himself in her. Her body was fuel to the simmering fire building inside him. Her lips were soft, welcoming, addictive.

Lifting her up, he set her on top of the island. Eventually, he had no choice but to pull back, breaking the kiss to breathe. With hooded eyes, she looked at him as he lifted her shirt up and off. The strap of her bra fell over her shoulder and he slowly pulled it down. He took her nipple in his mouth, circling it with his tongue and suckling until she cried his name. He swept his hands over the quivering skin of her stomach before he brushed his lips against her navel and dipped his tongue inside.

Love's head fell back as she sighed. "Drake, please."

He traced the waistband of her shorts with his tongue before pulling them off. He groaned, seeing the tiny piece of lace she had on underneath. After running his finger over the fabric, he gripped the elastic and pulled it off, leaving her exposed, open for him.

Drake dropped to his knees, brushed his finger over her slit. She was slick with yearning, writhing under his touch. He massaged her to a quick climax, enjoying her hoarse cries as her orgasm ripped through her. He didn't even give her a chance to come down from her high before he leaned in and tasted her, swirling his tongue around her clit before taking it in his mouth.

It didn't take long before she came again, this time so long and hard he had to fight his own release. But there was so much more he wanted to do. He wanted to take his time, love her thoroughly.

Standing, he cradled her in his arms and carried her into the living room. Laying her on the couch, he peered down at his satisfied wife. She was glorious, glowing. He unbuttoned his shirt and tugged it off.

Love reached out and unbuckled his belt, sliding it free. She unbuttoned his pants and tugged them and his boxers off. Her eyes flashed as she took in every inch of him, her palms smoothing over the muscles of his legs and lower abdomen before squeezing his erection.

Drake groaned before he grasped her wrists. "I don't want to come in your hand, baby. I want to come inside you."

Love fell back on the cushions, pulling him with her. Nestled between her legs, he kissed her forehead, her nose, then finally her mouth, biting down on her bottom lip as he pushed inside her. They started slow, familiarizing themselves with each other and finding a rhythm of their own. As they discovered their groove, the pace quickened and soon they were racing toward completion.

As much as he needed the release, Drake wanted to savor this moment. She was everything. And he was all hers. There was nobody else, no expectations or obligations. They were in sync with each other. He had never experienced anything even close to this, and he wanted it to last as long as possible before the weight of reality crashed down on them.

With that in mind, he whispered, "Let go."

That was all it took. He watched her as she came. It took everything in him not to let her milk his release from him. He bit the inside of his cheek as waves of pleasure washed over her.

A few seconds later, she opened her eyes and smiled. He felt a shift near his heart as his chest tightened. She was so damn beautiful.

She ran a knuckle down his cheek. "I can't believe we did this again."

Placing a finger over her lips, he said, "I'm not done with you yet."

Her eyes widened as he started moving again, thrusting in and out of her like there was no tomorrow full of explanations and excuses. This time, their lovemaking was slower, deliberate.

"Look at me," he commanded softly.

He knew he was close, but he wanted her with him when he came. With their gazes locked on each other, they found their release together.

Drake gave himself over to Love in more ways than one, and he knew there would be no turning back.

Drake woke the next morning still on the couch, with Love wrapped around him like a warm blanket. And he couldn't think of anywhere he'd rather be. Which, frankly, scared him to death.

"Drake?" Love's voice was soft, unsure. Definitely not groggy with sleep. "Are you awake?"

"Yes," he admitted.

She lifted herself up on an elbow. "We had sex again."

Sex? That was definitely not sex. Drake had had plenty of sex and none of it was even remotely similar to what had happened between him and Love. "Are you cold?"

She glanced at him. "Did you hear me?"

"I heard you," he murmured.

She fingered a fold in the throw he'd draped over them. "Can we talk about this?"

Not with your naked body pressed against mine. "Maybe we should get dressed."

Unfortunately, she didn't take the hint and move. "Drake, this isn't what I expected. We made love."

"Well, we are married." He knew his attempt at humor didn't work when her chin quivered. He squeezed the tip of it between his thumb and forefinger. "I'm sorry."

She dropped her forehead against his chest, and he tickled the back of her neck.

"It's complicated," she murmured. "We've yet to talk about this marriage and lawyers and the divorce. Instead, we had sex again. I'm worried we just changed things once more."

Their lovemaking had been intense, a game changer for him. And he definitely wasn't ready for the change. "Love, I'd like to think that we've been friends long enough to withstand anything that comes our way. We're adults, and we made an adult decision last night."

She glanced up at him. "What now?"

He brushed his thumb over her eyebrow. "I honestly don't know. And it's kind of hard to think about that when you're lying against me like this."

She laughed then. It was a full, throaty laugh that seemed to lodge itself in his heart. Love was beautiful on an average day, but the after-sex-relaxed-bedhead Love was stunning. She was perfect.

"You're my best friend," she said.

He swept his palm over her shoulder and squeezed. "Nothing is going to change that."

"You're worried."

"Who said I was worried?"

"You don't have to say it."

Distracted by her and the need to be with her again, he sat up. She held the blanket to her chest and slid off him so that he could stand. After dragging on his pants, he turned to her. "If I'm worried, it's because I don't want you hurt. Not because I'm worried about our friendship."

"We slept together, Drake. How do we come back from that? It's not like we can magically not be attracted to each other."

She stood and slipped on his shirt, which looked damn good on her. So good, he imagined taking her again with the shirt on. "We don't. We adjust to it. Like you said, we can't take it back. It's like an amputation. We'll miss the way it was before, but we'll learn to live differently."

"I say that to my patients who've just lost loved ones."

"I know," he said. "It applies here, too."

She chewed on her thumbnail. "What if it happens again?"

He'd asked himself the same question a million times since she'd put on that shirt. He knew it was going to happen again, he just didn't know when. "It won't," he lied. "We won't let it, okay?"

"And you can just go back to normal?"

Nope. "Well, I want to try to figure this out. You're too important to me not to try and work on it."

She walked closer, peered up at him with sad eyes. "Are you sure?"

He wrapped his arms around her, and she burrowed into him.

"I need you, Drake."

They stood like that for a while, swaying to their own music. "I'm here, Love. Always."

A hard knock at the door interrupted their tentative peace. Love frowned. "Who could that be? It's so early."

Drake buttoned Love up in his shirt. She smoothed a hand over her hair as he walked to the door. There was another knock before he got there and he paused when he saw who was on the other side through the small window. *Shit.*

"Who is it?" Love asked, tugging at his shirt.

Without answering her, he opened the door. "Mom."

"Mom?" he heard Love say behind him.

Gloria breezed into the condo like she owned the place. "Drake, you're here. Be a doll and grab my luggage. Lovely, I've been calling you."

"Mom, what are you doing here?" she asked.

Drake dragged the three heavy suitcases forward. "Are you moving in or something?" He met Love's mortified gaze.

"Silly," Gloria said with a grin. "No. I just wanted to spend more time with my daughter. I've finally decided to get that second opinion from a U of M doctor, like you've been suggesting. Plus, we have to get started on the wedding festivities."

The color drained from Love's face, and Drake walked over to her. *"Are you okay?"* he mouthed.

She placed a hand over her heart and shook her head. "Wait! Oh no," Gloria said with a gasp.

Drake looked at her. "What?" He followed Gloria's gaze toward the couch, then Love, then him, and realized she was connecting all the dots.

"Oh my," Gloria said, clasping her hand over her heart. "I'm sorry. I interrupted something."

Love glanced back at the couch and her eyes widened. "Mom—"

"It's cool, Lovely. You are newlyweds. I guess I should have booked a hotel room. It's just that usually I stay with you, and I was looking forward to bonding time."

"Mom, you know I don't have a problem with you staying here. It's just—"

"Oh good," Gloria said. "I'll just use the downstairs bedroom. You won't even know I'm here. I promise."

She pulled her cell phone out and placed a call. Drake and Love stood speechless as she connected with an old friend, made plans for dinner and gushed about her now married daughter. When Gloria clicked off, she yawned and announced she was going to take a nap because she hadn't been able to sleep on the red-eye.

It wasn't until they heard the slam of the downstairs bedroom door that Love said, "We're screwed."

Nodding, Drake said, "I know."

Chapter 10

The hospital elevator door opened and Love zoomed out and down the hall toward the lounge. She had to think. She was still married to Drake, and they hadn't even hired an attorney yet, hadn't talked about getting an annulment or divorce since they'd returned from Las Vegas. And her mother was there, staying with her—and Drake.

It had been a week since Gloria had shown up on her doorstep. Drake had moved in temporarily, to keep up appearances. Every night they'd retreated to bed together. Every morning Drake woke up, showered and dressed, leaving before the crack of dawn. Yes, they slept in the same room, but Drake had insisted on sleeping on the floor. She suspected he hadn't done much sleeping, but she hadn't called him on it. Things had gone quiet between them. A week before, he'd made her climax so many times the memories made her quiver with yearning. Yet they still hadn't resolved anything.

Love had kept busy carting her mother around during her off time. They'd already seen several specialists, and the diagnosis had been confirmed. It was peripheral artery disease, or PAD. Oftentimes, patients with PAD confuse their symptoms with neuropathy or something else entirely. As a result, it's often undiagnosed. In her mother's case, Gloria thought she was just "getting old" and failed to tell her doctors *all* of her symptoms.

They'd worked with a nutritionist on a diet plan that Love hoped would help control Gloria's diabetes. Next, they were set to see a surgeon to discuss the amputation recommendation that Gloria's Nevada doctor had given. The thought of her mother losing a foot and a leg made Love sick to her stomach, and she was willing to do anything possible to prevent it.

"Love?"

She froze, turning slowly. Derrick stood there smiling at her, with a bouquet of flowers in his hand. "What are you doing here?" she asked him.

He held the flowers out to her. "Peace offering?"

Love scanned the area, noting the interested glances from the nurses and other staff on the floor. The news of her marriage to Drake hadn't hit the hospital ticker yet, but she'd made it a practice of not bringing her personal life into the job. Every second of the day, a staff member was involved in some mess at their workplace. The hospital really was a den of scandal, fodder for the next television medical drama.

Derrick was dressed in a slim-fit blue suit with a

mini check pattern. He wore his clothes well, spending thousands on tailoring and ties. His slate watch and his bald head gleamed under the hospital lights. As he approached her, she instinctively backed up a step, needing to keep some distance between them.

He stopped in his tracks, lowering his extended hand and letting out a heavy sigh. "Can we go somewhere?" he asked under his breath.

Clutching the strap of her bag, she considered him for a moment. There was a time when she'd have done anything for Derrick. He was everything she'd thought she'd wanted in a man. They had the same goal of settling down in a suburban area and starting a family. While Drake dreamed of nightlife in the big city, Derrick was satisfied spending evenings at home, each of them working on their laptops next to each other on the couch. They'd been happy together. Well, she was happy. So happy that she'd never batted an eye when he'd announced he had taken an assignment in California for a year. She'd actually encouraged him to go follow his dream. The Harper family owned and operated a medical supply company. He'd spent years proving that he could take over the reins from his father, and it had paid off nicely when he'd stepped into the vice president of supply chain and logistics role, in their Michigan office.

As hurt as she'd been, she could look at him now and still see the amazing man he was. He'd made mistakes—a lot of them—but he wasn't a bad guy. Never had been. And she wasn't totally blameless in the downfall of their relationship. She'd promised monthly visits, but had canceled all of them due to some work thing or another. In reality, she'd been content in the long-distance relationship, and not inclined to make visiting him a priority. She'd been distracted with work and her patients. And he'd begged her for time. Eventually, he'd found someone who'd given him the time Love wouldn't.

It still didn't make it right that he'd cheated. Or the tactless way he'd ended it with her. The breakup had devastated her, knocked the wind out of her. He'd hurt her beyond words, and forgiveness was a long way off.

"Derrick, I think we've said all we have to say at this point. You made your choice. It's been a year, and you can't come waltzing back in here with a ring and flowers like you didn't break my heart."

The flowers were beautiful, though. The large, colorful arrangement featured a variety of blooms in magenta and orange, including several snapdragons, her favorite. Since they weren't in season, she figured he'd paid a pretty penny for the bouquet. The fragrance wafted to her nose, and she took the bouquet from him, inhaling the sweet scent. It reminded her of bubble gum. Memories of nights in her mother's greenhouse assaulted her. She'd spend hours inside, immersing herself in the different smells as she'd studied. It was her peaceful hiding place when her parents were divorcing. Drake had often met her there, held her as she'd cried.

The thought of Drake made her spine stiffen. He'd been so distant lately, and she felt helpless. So much had happened between them, it was hard to figure a way around everything.

"Love, please. Ten minutes. That's all I'm asking for," Derrick said.

"I know you want to talk, but it's not possible," she

told him. No matter what happened with Drake, she had to find a way to send Derrick away.

Sighing, she continued, "You worked with my father to manipulate me. Do you know how much trouble you've caused?"

Love hadn't seen her father since that day in his office. The day she'd defended Drake and their relationship before storming out. She had attempted to mend fences with her dad, but his secretary had informed her that he'd left town for a conference.

"That's why I wanted to talk to you," Derrick said. "I was wrong to go to your father. I was upset and jealous. During our relationship, you'd always told me you and Drake were only friends. I never believed that was all it was, but I dealt with it because I loved you and wanted a life with you. Then you *married* him, Love."

She glanced around to make sure no one was within earshot. The last thing she needed was to be the subject of the hospital rumor mill. Derrick had seemed skeptical when she'd described her friendship with Drake to him before. The two men had never really gotten along, which made it difficult in the beginning of their relationship. Derrick had told her several times that he thought Drake was in love with her, and she'd refuted his claims fervently.

"It made me rethink so many moments in our relationship," Derrick continued, shoving his hands into his pockets. "I want to believe that what we had was real, but seeing you with him, watching the closeness between you two, pissed me off. There is a level of understanding and acceptance between you that we never had. Part of me knew that's why you never really cared enough to visit me in California. You didn't need my companionship because you already had his. He fulfills that for you. Yes, I handled it all wrong. I hurt you, which was the last thing I ever wanted to do because I care for you so much. But you hurt me, too, Love."

His words hit her in her gut. Swallowing roughly, she nodded. "I know. But we can't go back and undo that now. Too much has happened."

Derrick bowed his head. "I still love you."

Before Love could respond, a voice came from behind her. "Unfortunately for you, that doesn't matter now."

Love whirled around. Drake was standing behind her, a chart in one hand and a cup of coffee in the other. "Drake? Where did you come from?"

He shot her a wary glance, before turning his attention to Derrick. "I know Love has told you to leave her alone. Yet you're still here. And with flowers this time. Where's the ring? Ready for a repeat of Vegas? Instead of a door slamming in your face, how about my fist?"

"Drake," Love croaked. "Stop."

But Drake wasn't paying her any attention. He was focused squarely on Derrick, his jaw set in determination and his eyes full of ire.

"I would comment, but I don't think you want to hear what I have to say," Derrick said.

"You're right, I don't want to hear anything you have to say."

Derrick stepped forward, his nostrils flared. "You don't want none, Drake. So I suggest you walk away."

Love gasped. Did Derrick just take it there? She

wedged herself between them. "Hey, please stop this. I'm at work."

"You heard her, Harper," Drake taunted. "We're at work. Go somewhere else, and take those damn flowers and that sorry-ass apology with you."

Derrick let out a humorless chuckle. "Feeling threatened?"

Drake shrugged. "Nah, man. I know the history between you two. All of it."

"You know nothing about me. I'm even going to venture to say you don't really know anything about my relationship with Love. Maybe a few things, but not everything. You forget, I know Love, too. She's not the type to share everything."

Drake frowned, caught her gaze for a minute. His eyes softened a bit before he turned a hard glare back toward Derrick. "I know all I need to know, and let me tell you something *you* may not know. I don't care about the relationship you and Love *had*. I just care that you know it's over."

"Maybe," Derrick said simply.

"Definitely," Drake countered. "At the end of the day, you're standing here proposing a reconciliation with *my* wife. And you don't see the problem with this?"

Love vaguely registered the whispers around her. She met the eyes of several of the staff around her, as they registered the "tea" that Drake just poured. Her days of flying under the radar at work were over.

"Drake," she muttered under her breath. "We have an audience."

He peered down at her, a small smile on his lips. "I know," he said. "I don't care."

"I care," she snapped. "We have to work here."

His jaw tightened. "Fine. Handle this, then." He motioned toward Derrick. "Because if you don't, I will."

Drake turned to leave, but she gripped his wrist, halting his retreat. "Don't go. We need to talk."

"Not here, and not in front of him."

Sighing, Love glanced at Derrick. "You have to go."

"Can we meet for coffee later?" he asked.

"No, she can't." Drake's voice was louder this time. "You don't want this kind of problem with me, man. If you don't get the hell away from her—"

Love whirled around, her eyes darting about the floor. She knew what that meant. Although Drake was from a wealthy family, he'd been in several fights in high school due to his hot temper. The boys had tended to try him because they'd thought he was a soft rich boy who would take it. "Drake, go in the lounge. I'll handle this, and we'll talk." When he didn't move, she added, searching his eyes, "Please."

The kiss that followed caught her off guard. It wasn't sweet; rather, it was hard and possessive. His tongue pushed past her lips, and his hands were in her hair, holding her to him. She moaned as he devoured her mouth with passion in front of the entire floor. She felt that kiss from the top of her head to the tips of her toes. Electricity sizzled around them and she had no choice but to give in to his demanding mouth. Then it was over and he was walking away from her.

On shaky legs, she looked up at Derrick, handing him the flowers. "I'm sorry, Derrick. You have to go. Drake is my husband, and you need to respect that."

Pivoting on her heels, she took a steadying breath, and left Derrick standing there.

Drake paced the lounge area, after kicking everybody out. The last person, one of his colleagues, had just scurried off when Love walked in, locking the door behind her.

"Drake, what the hell was that?"

He didn't have an answer for his behavior. The only thing he knew was the blinding jealousy, the burning sensation in his chest, when he'd encountered the two of them standing so close together. The flowers in her hands, and the way she'd looked at the other man. Despite what Love had said, it was obvious to him that she still felt something for Derrick. Just thinking about it made his stomach clench.

He'd been reckless, confronting Derrick the way he had in front of the staff, his colleagues. It would be fodder for the gossips for weeks, but he didn't care at that moment. The only thing he'd cared about was putting his fist through Derrick's face.

"Drake?" Love's voice pulled him out of his thoughts. "Talk to me."

He shook his head, resuming his rapid pacing back and forth. "I can't right now."

"Why are you so angry?"

"Why aren't *you* angry? He doesn't even deserve your time, but you gave him plenty of it today."

She recoiled as if he'd slapped her, her hand flying to her mouth. "How long… What do you think you saw, Drake?"

"It doesn't matter. You were falling for it, even though you didn't want to."

"I wasn't. I told him to leave, that too much had happened."

He'd heard her words, but he could read her better than she knew. He knew when Love was wavering, when she was doubting herself and her decision, and when she was attracted to someone. He'd seen the way she eyed Derrick as he approached, the appreciation in her eyes. It had taken every ounce of restraint in him not to kick the retractable banner about cardiac health that he'd cowered behind in order to eavesdrop. Eventually, he hadn't been able to take it anymore and had stepped forward, if only to let the other man know that Love was off-limits.

"Listen, Love. Whether you believe it or not, he won't give up. And you know why? Because you gave him an ear, you accepted his peace offering and engaged in a trip down memory lane."

Realization dawned in her pretty brown eyes. They were eyes that had haunted his dreams in the past week, made him retreat inward to deal with the gamut of emotions he'd experienced since he'd made love to her a second time.

"I told you," she said. "Everything is different between us. And you promised it wouldn't be."

Averting his gaze, he studied the scratch on the tile, the one he and Love had put there months ago when they were moving the heavy table to the other side of the room.

"We have to talk about this, Drake."

His heartbeat quickened when she grabbed his hand and squeezed. When he looked into her eyes, he knew he was lost. She was right; everything had changed. He couldn't pretend anymore that he didn't want her. "I can't do this right now, Love. Seriously."

He glanced at his watch. His worst fears had been realized when he'd been relegated to scrubbing in on appendectomies. Before Dr. Leon knew he'd married his daughter, Drake had been on track to scrub in with Dr. Benjamin Porter on an off pump coronary artery bypass surgery. Instead, Love's father had assigned another less skilled resident to the coveted spot.

Love's chin trembled and she stared down at her hands.

Guilt slammed into Drake like a Mack truck. "I'm sorry," he mumbled. "We'll talk. Just not here. We can have dinner tonight, and discuss it."

She bit her lip. "I can cook, if you'd like."

Drake had managed to avoid being in the kitchen alone with her over the past week. He didn't think he wanted to take the chance of showing his ass again this soon. "Maybe we can go out to our spot."

The Mexican restaurant by the mall was their favorite place to eat out. Love was enamored with the gooey queso dip, and he appreciated the strong drinks. He definitely needed a stiff one if they were actually going to have this conversation.

She smiled, and he found himself responding with one of his own. He leaned in, as if he didn't have any control of himself.

"Drake." The way she said his name, a mixture of a soft whisper and a groan, made him want to pin her on that table and make love to her right then and there.

"Love," he said, his voice low and unrecognizable even to his own ears. He swallowed past a lump that had wedged itself in his throat.

"Your phone is ringing."

He jerked back, pulling his phone off its clip. He'd been so entranced that he hadn't even felt the vibration. The 911 on the screen was his cue to exit. "I have to go." Good thing, too. There was no telling what would have happened if they hadn't been interrupted by the page. "Meet me at the spot at five o'clock?"

She smiled when he pinched her chin. "I will. See you soon."

Hours later, Drake was on his way to meet Love when he heard a familiar voice call his name. His day had sucked. The afternoon spent in the emergency department intubating patients had put him in a sour mood. But he'd rather be flipping burgers than dealing with the man behind him.

"I see you're on your way out," Dr. Lawrence Jackson said. "Don't you have some time for your father?"

Drake turned to face him. "Dad. What brings you here?"

Although his father was on staff at the University Hospital, he'd been traveling in recent years, consulting on cases at several top hospitals and delivering fiery speeches at medical schools across the nation.

"You would know why I'm here if you'd answer my many phone calls."

Drake's father wasn't one for a random check-in call or visit. There was always a reason behind his actions. Drake had spent most of his childhood avoiding the man, especially once he'd realized that nothing he did would ever be good enough for him. He'd worked his butt off in school, graduating at the top of his class at every stage of his education. But because he'd cho-

sen to explore cardiothoracic surgery instead of join-
ing the family specialty, his plastic surgeon father had
made it clear that he had no use for him.

"I'm busy," he told him. "Boards are soon, and I've
been preparing for them."

"And getting married."

Drake paused, unsure how to respond. He guessed
the gossip mill had churned all day after his display
earlier. "Dad, can we talk about this later? I'm on my
way to meet Love."

"Your wife." His father shook his head slowly, staring at him with a stony expression in his eyes. That
familiar look of disappointment seemed etched on
his face. "When did you decide to ruin your life and
career, son?"

Drake sighed heavily. "What makes you think I've
done that?"

His father explained the phone call he'd received
from Love's dad earlier in the week. The two had actually conversed about the "monumental" mistake
their offspring had made in getting married. Dr. Leon
had apparently gone on about how Love was his baby
girl and he didn't want Drake breaking his daughter's heart.

"Is she pregnant?" his father asked.

Drake shook his head. "Are you crazy? No."

He regretted his words and tone the minute he'd
used them. But his dad tended to take him there. Every
lecture, every criticism served to put him on the edge
of a small window ledge.

"Watch your mouth," Dr. Jackson warned.

Drake shifted, rubbing the back of his neck. "Why

would you even say that? That would imply that I only married her because she's having my baby."

"I had to ask. Leon is wealthy, but he's not of my stature."

His father's air of superiority rankled Drake. There were all these unwritten rules for a Jackson. Too bad there weren't rules against knocking up a woman that's not your wife, then basically paying her to give up custody of her child to his unfeeling father. That's what Dr. Lawrence Jackson had done to Drake's mother, after all. And although he'd never had the chance to really know his mother, Drake had always imagined how different his life would have been if his father wasn't such a domineering jerk.

The only contact he'd had with his mother's family was a maternal grandmother who'd visit from time to time. Grammy had been a breath of fresh air for Drake and when she'd died of a heart attack, he had become fascinated with the heart. It was that experience that lead him to declare his desire to go into cardiothoracic surgery, to the utter displeasure of his controlling father.

"Dad, you like Love."

That much was true. His father, always one to point out everyone's flaws, had never given him any indication that he didn't like Love. In fact, he'd doted on her when they were near each other, offering her drinks and laughing heartily with her.

"Oh, I think she's a lovely person. But I don't agree with this farce of a marriage. Especially if it is going to hamper your ambitions. Leon already told me he moved you from a few key surgeries as a result."

"And what did you say to him?"

Heaven forbid, his father would actually defend him. Drake and his siblings were an afterthought, a means to an end. As long as they did what he told them. His younger twin brothers were also surgical residents, studying plastic surgery. And his youngest sibling, his sister, was in her final year of undergraduate studies at University of Michigan. Her goal? To become a part of the family's thriving plastic surgery practice. Drake and El were the only two who'd deviated from that preordained plan. El had chosen to go into emergency psychiatry.

The Jackson family was a pillar in the Ann Arbor area. His father and grandfather had perfected the art of philanthropy and had spent countless hours and dollars building up the family name. Drake's dad had moved to Las Vegas for work, and had honed his reputation in the health care field, having privileges in several Vegas area hospitals.

When Drake graduated from high school, his father decided to move back to Ann Arbor, even though he was rarely in town.

"Actually, I suggested that he get out of his feelings and reinstate you to your rightful place on the surgical resident team," his father told him. "I will not have him jeopardizing your career over this unfortunate mistake."

The word *mistake* lodged in Drake's head. The thought that his father considered Love a mistake made him want to smack him. "Don't call her that. She's not a mistake."

"I didn't call *her* a mistake." His father checked his watch. "There is a fund-raising event next week.

They are honoring me with an award. You are ex-pected to attend."

There it was. The real reason for his visit. "I can't be there," Drake told him.

"You will be there. It's not a request. On Monday, Leon wants to meet us for lunch. I told him you'd be there, as well. Get out of your feelings, and do what you need to do to get to where you want to be. Listen, I wasn't particularly happy when you defied my wishes, but you are still better than any of those in-competent residents in the general surgery program. You have a fellowship to win at Johns Hopkins, and intubating patients and performing appendectomies won't cut it."

Drake scanned the area, catching a few curious glances from others. "I have to go."

"To dinner with me," his father said smoothly. "I have a late flight and we have business to discuss."

The man strolled toward the elevators, winking at a nurse and giving a curt nod to another doctor, be-fore turning expectantly to Drake.

Reluctantly, Drake followed him, sending Love a quick text, letting her know he'd see her at home later.

Chapter 11

Love rubbed her eyes and craned her neck toward the sound of her blaring phone. Frowning, she reached over to the nightstand to answer it. Only it wasn't there. The ringing continued. She opened an eye and noticed the flashing light coming from her open purse, in the chair. *Damn*.

She silently prayed that whoever was calling wasn't dying, because she had no intention of getting out of bed to answer it. Jumping, she pitched a pillow toward the offensive sound and covered her face with another one.

When the ringing stopped, she thanked God and pulled the comforter over her head. Unfortunately, the caller was persistent, and the phone sounded again. Love rolled out of bed and landed on her butt. Growling, she crawled over to her purse, dumped the contents on the floor and grabbed the phone. "What?" she yelled.

"Lovely Grace Washington!"

Oh, my God. "Hello? Hello?" She pushed the end button and hung up on her father. More than likely he wouldn't fall for the lost signal excuse she was about to give him, but she wasn't prepared to talk to him, especially after their last conversation. She needed to gather her thoughts.

She glanced at the mound of folded blankets on the small love seat at the far end the room. Drake wasn't home yet and it was—she glanced at the clock—11:00 p.m. Earlier that evening he had canceled their dinner with a simple text and nothing else. Now awake, she tiptoed down the stairs to the living room, then the kitchen, hoping she wouldn't wake her mother who was in the downstairs bedroom. No Drake.

Where the hell is he?

Love hurried to the bathroom and turned on the shower. She'd fallen asleep waiting for Drake, and now she was concerned that he hadn't called. After trying his cell a few times, and getting his voice mail, she decided to go to the hospital to see if he was there.

Stepping into the hot shower, she moaned. The water felt so good against her weary skin, but she had to make it quick. Her father was bound to call back any minute and she had no choice but to talk to him.

Once she finished, she stepped out and wrapped a huge bath sheet around her. Turning to the mirror, she wiped the condensation off and ran a comb through her hair.

"Love?" Drake called from the other side of the door.

She flung it open. "You're here."

He swept his gaze over her body, then turned away. "What are you doing up?"

She grabbed his arm and drew him back. "I was going to head to the hospital to find you. My father called. I hung up on him."

"You what?"

"Where were you? I tried to call you a few times."

"My father showed up at the hospital, and we went to dinner. Argued a little, then I went back to the hospital to check on a patient before I came here."

A pang of guilt shot through her. She knew Drake had a volatile relationship with his dad, and that the older man's visits often ended with a bad argument. "I'm sorry. What is he in town for?"

"Fund-raising event." Drake shook his head. "And you should know your father called him."

A heavy feeling settled in her stomach, and she leaned against the bathroom sink. "Wow. My dad certainly didn't waste any time. How did that conversation go?"

"Well, they both agree that we made a mistake in getting married. Both feel that our decision is detrimental to our careers. Basically, your father doesn't think I'm good enough for you, and neither of them believes that we're capable of living our lives without their guidance and instruction."

She pulled her towel tighter against her chest. Swallowing, she said, "Drake, I'm so… I feel like this is my fault. After all this time, I've tried to give my dad the benefit of the doubt, but he's not the same man that I grew up with. He's controlling and dismissive.

He shouldn't have said the things he did to you, or your father."

"You are not to blame for your father's actions, just like I'm not for mine."

"I know it hurts you, because you care about him." Love knew the respect and admiration Drake had for her father. Learning that none of that mattered now had to be a blow. "I'm so angry with him."

"Don't be," Drake said. "You can't control his reaction. But we do need to talk about this. And not just gloss over it."

"Do you want something to drink? Or eat?"

He shook his head. "Not really." He tugged his shirt off and shuffled into the bathroom. "My father has requested our appearance at the high society fundraiser next Saturday. He's getting an award, and has to make it appear that the Jackson family is loving and supportive of each other."

"Well, I'm not coming to that."

He looked over at her. "I know you hate events like this, but I need you there."

Love's stance softened at Drake's sincerity. She knew it would be hard for him to be around his father, in the type of environment that always made him feel like a fake. He'd grown up feeling like he was "daddy's little secret," and Dr. Lawrence Jackson had never done much to correct that assumption.

His siblings were cool, and Love enjoyed hanging out with all of them. But they didn't have the same baggage as Drake because they were born of marriage, albeit marriages to different women.

Dr. Law, as Love called him, had been married three times. The twins were born to his first wife.

His arrival in the home had caused many a problem, because Drake was the result of a torrid affair. Dr. Jackson's wife at the time resented Drake, even though he was not to blame for the heartache she'd suffered. She'd made life hell for him, and that's why Love was so grateful for her loving mother, who'd never hesitated to show Drake love and understanding.

Drake was proof that money wasn't everything. His life was anything but charmed, even though he was born with wealth and status simply because he had the last name Jackson.

Love relented. "I'll be there."

"Thank you."

"I know how you feel about your father. This is the worst possible time for him to be in town, while we're trying to figure things out."

"Yeah, well, it is what it is."

Drake made quick work of brushing his teeth and washing his face. And Love found herself staring at his broad, well-defined shoulders, his ripped back, his strong arms, and toned abs. His pants hung low on his hips, giving her a glimpse of the thin line of hair disappearing under the waistband of his black boxer briefs.

"Do you still want to talk?" he asked. The smirk on his full lips let her know that he'd caught her staring. Again.

Eyeing the door, and rubbing a hand through her wet hair, she answered, "Um, sure."

His slow, deliberate gaze over her body sent a shiver of awareness to her core. "Don't you think you should put on some clothes?" She opened her mouth to respond, but stopped short when he added, "Or I could take mine off so we're equal."

She let out a nervous laugh and stepped away from him, tripping over a shoe in the middle of the floor and tumbling backward. She landed with a loud thud on her butt. Jumping up, she struggled to regain her composure as behind her, she heard Drake chuckle. Her face and neck burned as she entertained the idea of bolting. She couldn't turn around and face him. Her chest tightened, and a tingle swept up the back of her neck and across her cheeks. Rubbing her arms, she took in a deep breath.

He wasn't laughing anymore. In fact, the room was too quiet. Love leaned against her dresser and listened for any sign of Drake in the room behind her. She heard him draw closer to her, until he was right behind her. She smelled the faint scent of his soap and the minty toothpaste he'd just used.

She felt his nose against the back of her neck, then his lips as he brushed them against her sensitive skin.

"I'm sorry," he muttered, pressing another kiss to her back. "I shouldn't have laughed. I think I like that I make you nervous."

"It's not funny, Drake."

"You're right. It's not a laughing matter."

Instinctively, she knew he wasn't talking about her fall anymore. He confirmed that when he whispered, "You're driving me insane, Love. This past week has been torture for me, staying in this room only a few feet away from you, not touching you like I want to."

"I didn't know what you were thinking," she admitted. "We barely saw each other. You disappeared on me, and it scared me."

He rested his chin on her shoulder. "I know. It scares me, too."

It was unlike him to be so vulnerable with anyone. She hated that their situation was pulling them both out of their normal routine with each other. There had never been any awkwardness between them. She was never nervous around him. But now...

"You smell so good," he breathed against her skin, before sucking her earlobe into his mouth.

"Thank you," she whispered.

His soft laugh made her hot, and the way his hands roamed her body ignited the fire. He picked up her hand and kissed the back of it. "I want you."

She let out a shaky breath. The admission sent her heart soaring right over the cliff edge she'd been holding on to as if her life depended on it. She was falling hard for her husband, and her emotions frightened her with their intensity.

"Drake, we should probably talk, like we said we would."

He squeezed her hips, brushed his erection against her butt. "I know we should, but...it's very hard to do that when all I want to do is make love to you."

"Maybe we should sit on opposite sides of the room?" she suggested.

Drake sighed and retreated to a chair on the other side of the bed. "You're right. Let's do this, because we really should deal with it."

She couldn't figure out if he was being sarcastic or serious, especially since she hadn't looked at him yet. Reluctantly, she turned around to face him. His eyes were dark, almost black as he assessed her. The heat in them scorched her already tingling skin.

Pulling on the robe that was lying on her bed, she shimmied out of the towel, tied the belt around her waist and sat down. "Okay, where do we start?"

"With the obvious," he replied. "We had sex."

He'd finally said the word without averting his gaze. She smiled to herself. "Really?" she asked sarcastically.

"That's where we should begin." He glared at her. "We've been friends for years. Why now? What made that night different?"

"I don't know," she murmured, crossing her legs. Earlier, at the hospital, after the confrontation with Derrick, she'd taken a moment to really look at him. The Drake she knew would have never let someone push his buttons the way Derrick had. "I wish I knew."

"Me, too. It's not like we've had underlying feelings for each other, near kisses or almost moments over the years. It was out of left field."

"I've seen you checking me out."

His eyes flashed to hers. "What are— I didn't. I mean, I've appreciated the gifts God gave you, but I didn't want to do you."

She shrugged. "Well, I think you're an attractive man. So it's not that far out of the realm of possibilities."

"I want us to be okay, Love. I almost could have believed we'd be good after the whole marriage and wedding night. But this week, that night…it was a choice we both made to go there again. I'm not so sure we can be all right after this."

Her stomach rolled. "But you said—"

"I know what I said, Love. I married you while we were both intoxicated, and we got busy like we had no care in the world or concern for the consequences. That was bad enough, but I seduced you in your kitchen the next week. I kissed you in front of our coworkers. You went against your father for me. I can't wrap my head around this. I feel like I'm the bad guy that your dad thinks I am because I couldn't see past what I wanted for the good of our friendship."

"Wait, I'm a grown ass woman, Drake. You didn't make me have sex with you."

"You're sweet. You're like Little Red Riding Hood."

"And you're the Big Bad Wolf?"

"Exactly." He threw his hands in the air.

She giggled. "Come on, Drake. You're not some predator luring sweet little ole' me into your lair for a little dessert and some cookies."

"You're smiling again. And this isn't funny."

"It is funny." She scooted closer to him, until she was in front of him. Kneeling before him, she placed her hands on top of his. "I was a willing participant in everything, including the other night. I wanted you, just like I wanted you a few minutes ago. Now if you ask me why, again, I don't know."

"It was good, Love. I want it again, too."

She felt a blush creep up her face. "Yeah, it was. I think it's because we were in sync with each other, which isn't new. We always work well together."

He frowned. "That's a weird way of looking at it."

"Well, I've had a lot of time to think about it, while you were avoiding me."

"I don't know what to say."

There really was nothing to say, Love mused. He stroked a finger over her brow, and she leaned into his touch as he caressed her face. "That's the problem.

We can't change what happened, or even explain why. We just know that we both enjoyed each other, and we'll remember this for the rest of our lives. What we should talk about is our next step. How are we going to move forward?"

"How do you propose we do that when we're sleeping in close quarters? The attraction is palpable."

"I guess the real question is, are we going to stop?"

His eyes widened, then narrowed. "Do you want to stop?"

She bit her lip, tucked a stray hair behind her ear. The answer to that question was an enthusiastic "no." But she couldn't say that to him. Could she?

"Let's sleep on it," she said instead. "We don't want to make another rash decision."

He seemed to accept her answer. "Right. Well, I'm going to go downstairs and do some work." He stood, and helped her to her feet. Her robe fell open and she closed it quickly. He fingered the opening, brushing his knuckle over her nipple. "Don't sleep in that. In fact, why don't you wear those ugly ass pajamas you bought last Christmas with the feet in them?"

She laughed. He'd teased her mercilessly about her bunny pajamas. She'd found them at Macy's and couldn't resist. Apparently, they were coming back in style. "That would be a no. I haven't worn them again because they're so hot."

"Like the woman wearing them."

Her breath caught in her throat. "You're making me high."

He offered her a bemused smile. "Join the club." He leaned and whispered against her ear, "You don't want to know what I'm thinking right now. So I'm going to go downstairs. I'll see you in the morning."

Love was getting whiplash from the back and forth between them. But she'd happily buckle up for the ride if it meant preserving what was best about them. She couldn't live without him.

Chapter 12

The sound of Love's alarm interrupted a steamy dream about Drake. She sat upright in the bed, and noted the empty room. Disappointed that Drake had disappeared on her again, she hurriedly dressed and made her way downstairs quietly. She didn't want to wake her mother at four thirty in the morning, but she had a busy day ahead. Besides work, today was the appointment with her mother's surgeon.

In the kitchen, Love pulled a travel mug out of the cabinet and inserted a K-cup into the Keurig.

"You're up early."

She yelped, holding her hands to her chest. "Drake? You scared me. What are you doing up?"

He stood and stretched. "Fell asleep studying."

The smell of caramel, vanilla and coffee filled the room, and her mouth watered. Love was a coffee girl.

Having her morning cup of joe really was the best part of her day. She picked up her mug and replaced it with an empty one. "You want a cup?"

Drake nodded. "Thanks."

She put two slices of bread into the toaster and pulled out the peanut butter from the pantry. "Breakfast?"

"Nah. I'll grab something on my way to work."

"Sure? I can scramble a couple eggs for you."

He moistened his lips, held eye contact with her for a minute, before turning away. "I'm good. It's too early."

She held his mug, filled with his favorite breakfast blend, out to him. He took his coffee black. She shivered at the spark that passed between them when their fingers touched as he took the offered cup of coffee.

Clearing her throat, she told him, "I've been thinking about our fathers. We're doing the right thing, sticking together. They can't know the sordid details of our wedding. It would just make matters worse."

With her mug in her hand, she blew on the coffee and took a sip. She'd planned to have a talk with her dad today, to make sure he knew where she stood.

"I agree. What happens when we file for an annulment or divorce?"

She snorted, doubting a judge would grant them an annulment now. The only thing in their favor was they were both intoxicated at the time. But even then, their history would make it hard. "Have you thought about which attorney you want to use? Maybe we can use Jared?"

He rolled his eyes. "No."

Jared Williams was a friend that she'd met when

she'd treated his twin sister, Sydney. She'd just broken up with Derrick, and "Red" had been charming and attentive. It was exactly what she'd needed at the time, but it didn't go anywhere, since Red was hopelessly in love with another woman.

"You do know that nothing ever happened between me and Red, right?"

"That's beside the point," Drake said with a shrug. "Red doesn't even practice family law. Why would we use him?"

Love sighed. It was foolish to hope there was a tiny bit of jealousy on Drake's part. She should have known he was being his practical self when he'd dismissed Red so quickly. "Right," she muttered under her breath. "Do you want me to ask him if he can suggest someone?"

"You could. Are we in a rush?"

The loaded question caught her off guard. "I don't know. You brought it up, so…"

"I asked a question, Love." His gaze locked on her as he took a sip of his coffee. It felt like a caress, like his hands were on her, touching her body. "I'm not saying I want to go out and hire someone right this second. We have a lot to consider. For one, my job. I haven't seen any real action in the OR since we made this announcement. Even though your father doesn't like us being married, I feel like if we get a divorce, he will really believe that I took advantage of you."

"Is that the only reason?" She tapped her fingernails against her mug and braced herself for his answer. They'd only agreed on the fact that they were attracted to each other. Staying married was another story.

He set his mug down on the counter. "Take off your clothes," he commanded softly, prying her mug from her clutches and setting it on the countertop, along with his.

She opened her mouth to protest even as she unbuttoned her shirt. No words followed, just soft breathing from both of them. Apparently, she wasn't moving fast enough, because he grabbed the waist of her jeans and pulled her to him to finish. He pulled her shirt off slowly, then unzipped her pants and peeled them off at an even slower pace. It was almost like torture, and he knew it. Love wanted to beg him to rip them off. Her body was on fire for him, needing him, wanting him.

He leaned his forehead against hers. "You're so damn beautiful. I don't know if I'll ever grow tired of touching you, kissing you."

"You haven't kissed me yet."

He caught her bottom lip with his mouth, lingering there before moving to her top lip. They shared short, soft kisses for a few seconds before it grew more frantic, with tongue and teeth and groans and hisses. She held him to her, her fingers gripping his scalp as she fought to stay on her feet. He made her legs weak, her mind cloudy, but she was all in.

She pulled his shirt off and pushed his pants down. "Drake, I want this," she murmured against his mouth. "Make love to me. Now."

He released the band holding her hair up, and her curls fell over her shoulders. Sweeping them to the side, he bit down on her neck, before sucking the tender spot until she had to stifle a cry. Somewhere in the haze of desire she remembered her mother asleep in the guest room. But not for long. As Drake blazed a trail of kisses up her neck, to her jawline, her chin, then her mouth, she could think of nothing but him. His arm wrapped around her like a steel band, and lifted her against him, coaxing her to wrap her legs around his waist. This time, instead of taking her to the couch, he carried her up the stairs to the bedroom, kissing her the entire way.

The taste of him made her dizzy with need. Her mind screamed to stop this before they ruined everything, but her heart and her body wanted him.

Gently, he lowered her to the bed, brushing fingertips over her trembling skin. Drake was the musician and she was his instrument, and he played her like an expert. He knew her, remembered the places that made her squirm with pleasure. Kissing her below her ear, he whispered, "Tell me how you want it."

Love wasn't shy, but she'd never taken the lead in lovemaking. She'd been content to let her partner take control. Drake made her want to please him, because he'd spent so much time making sure she was satisfied.

"How about you tell me?" she asked, arching her brow. "What do *you* want?"

He rested between her legs, ran his tongue over her parted lips. The hard evidence of his arousal pressed against her inner thigh. "You. That's all."

Love searched his eyes. There was no hesitation, no doubt. His hand slipped between them, into her wet heat. Her mouth fell open with a soundless cry as he circled her clit with his thumb, teased her, tempted her. Her hips rocked against his hand as his finger slid in and out of her. She was so wet for him, so gone. The pleasure took her over, warmed her from the inside.

She needed a release, and it didn't take long for her to spiral out of control and fall over the cliff as a climax tore through her body.

Love burrowed into the soft mattress, sated and drowsy. She placed a kiss on his neck, ran her tongue over the bulging vein that signaled his struggle to hold on, to not push forward inside her. His head fell to her shoulder and she tickled the hair at his nape, hugging him to her.

Seconds later, as he placed wet kisses against her ear, her shoulder and the base of her neck, she opened her eyes. He stared down at her, a sexy smile on his lips that seemed to ignite the ache between her thighs. She was consumed by him, as if he'd crawled inside her and taken over her body and soul. She wanted more, needed it to survive, like she needed sunlight or water.

As if he'd read her mind, he smoothed a hand down her side, over her waist to her knee, and raised it to wrap around his hip. Gripping her leg, he rested his length against her opening. She pushed up, tried to take him in, but he didn't move.

"Drake, please."

"Tell me how you want it," he repeated.

"I… I don't know."

The tip of his rock-hard erection pressed against her. "Love." His mouth met hers again in a soft feather of a kiss. It was vulnerable, needy. "I *need* you to say it."

The way he'd said her name, the way he implored her to tell him how she wanted to be loved, shook her resolve. There was a longing there she hadn't noticed before. Drake needed her to give him permission, to make it okay to love her in this way.

The line they'd crossed a couple weeks ago was gone. There was nothing standing between them, nothing in their way. She could give in and let this be what it was, or deny him. It was her choice, always her choice.

"Love." His hand tangled in her hair, pulled gently, urging her to make the decision.

Swallowing, she kissed his chin, then nipped it with her teeth. "I want you nice and slow."

She cried out as he filled her, the sound muffled by his mouth over hers in a demanding and passionate kiss. He held still, giving her a chance to adjust to his size, before telling her, "Your wish is my command."

An hour later, they lay joined together in a tangle of limbs. Love was nestled against Drake, her face against his chest. "I'm so late for my shift."

She felt the rumble of laughter underneath her cheek. "No, you're not. You're always two hours early. You still have time."

Propping herself up on her elbow, she kissed him. "I better go," she said against his mouth. "I have to shower again and get over to the hospital."

"I won't be there for a few hours."

"Can I ask you a question?"

He cocked his head to the side, raising his eyebrows. "You have to ask?"

Love ran her thumbnail over a scar on his chest. "Yes, I do. This is a serious one."

Drake groaned. "No, we can't go all serious lying in bed naked. I don't want to ruin the moment."

She sat up, holding the thin sheet against her body. "I have to ask."

He held her hand, ran his finger over the pulse point in her wrist. "Go ahead."

"Drake, I hate that your father makes you feel the way he does. Have you ever considered telling him how you really feel?"

"He already knows, Love."

"How could he?"

"I told him, when I was a senior in high school. I found out he'd never stopped sleeping with my mother. He'd lied to me for years, allowed me to believe that he had no connection to her and didn't know how to get in touch with her. They'd seen each other every single time he visited Reno, or she came to Vegas. And that wasn't even the worst part. He supported her financially, all the way up until she died."

"What?" A weight settled in her gut at his admission. "How could he?"

"Trust me, I've asked myself that same question many times since then." Drake explained that the argument started when Dr. Law broke the news of Drake's mother's death. It had spiraled from there, with the two men almost coming to blows. "The worst part was he didn't see where he was wrong. Still doesn't."

Drakes eyes watered, and her heart broke for him. She thought back to that time. Drake had been angry, withdrawn. She'd assumed it was grief over never knowing his mother and hadn't pushed him to open up to her. "I'm so sorry."

"There is nothing for you to be sorry for."

She felt the anguish radiating off of him, the despair at finding out that his mother had been in touch with his father but had never reached out to Drake. "I blame her, too. She could have demanded to see you. All those years, she had access to you and didn't take it."

Love climbed on top of him and hugged him. When his arms wrapped around her tightly, she closed her eyes. Love wasn't sure what she'd say to Dr. Law when she saw him again. She just knew that she wouldn't let him make Drake feel bad for being himself.

"It hurt," he confessed, his voice cracking. "I hated him for it. I lived in that house feeling like I was his dirty little secret, that I would never be good enough for him. He'd told me all these horror stories about my mother, and I accepted what he'd said because I didn't know her. He lied to me over and over, didn't even think he owed me the truth." Drake kissed Love's her forehead.

"Well, that's on him. He did owe you the truth, Drake. And you are good enough."

She looked at him then. Tears welled in her eyes and their gazes held. He brushed a tear from her cheek. "You know why I believe that now?"

"Why?"

"Because of you. You have always seen the best in me, been my biggest cheerleader. The support you've given me is invaluable. I don't know what I would have done without you." Another tear fell. "That's why we can't let whatever this is get between us."

"We won't," he vowed. "We can't."

An hour later, Drake sat in the living room drinking another cup of coffee. Love had left only a few minutes earlier, after he'd bared his soul to her and made love to her again.

They'd turned another corner that morning, lying in each other's arms. He'd shared something with her that he'd never told another person, and it felt good to be honest with someone about his mother and father.

Drake had never been an insecure person, except when his father was involved. It had taken him a lot of years to get over the revelation that his mother just never wanted him. The fact that she could willingly sleep with a married man while ignoring her own kid made him grateful that he'd never gotten to know her. He was certain she would have destroyed his life if she'd been a part of it.

"Hey, Drake," Gloria said, entering the room. He smiled at his surrogate mother. Gloria was beautiful, full of life. He remembered how fast she used to move when they were children. She'd never stop moving, always picking up extra jobs and making sure she was in the right places.

The Gloria of old was in stark contrast to the woman in front of him. Her gray hair was neat and she still had that gleam in her eyes, but her steps were slower. She wasn't moving as fast, due to her limp. Love had explained what was going on, and he'd agreed to drive Gloria to the hospital that morning for her appointment.

Diabetes was controllable, but it could be debilitating. He prayed that Gloria wouldn't have to lose a limb.

"Hey, Mom." He stood and helped her to the couch. "How are you feeling?"

"Well, I've seen better days, son."

"I figured we'd stop and get breakfast on the way to the hospital. Is that okay with you?"

The older woman smiled. "You don't have to put yourself out. Besides, I don't have much of an appetite. They've got me on a new medicine, and it's making me queasy."

Concerned, Drake asked, "Did you tell your doctor?"

She shook her head. "Not yet. I plan to mention it today. We have a call scheduled for after my appointment with the surgeon."

Drake wondered if Gloria would consider moving to Michigan. He knew Love would feel better if she was closer. But he suspected Gloria would rather walk over hot coals than move here, especially since her business was thriving. She'd had to trust her shop to her employees for once. Knowing Gloria, that had to be hard on her. He couldn't say he blamed her for not wanting to move, though. It wasn't his ideal place, and definitely not somewhere he'd planned on staying.

"Make sure you keep me posted. I'm glad you're here, though. I feel better knowing that you're getting a second opinion."

Drake had never understood how she'd fallen in love with Dr. Leon. They were nothing alike. Gloria was quirky and spontaneous, while Love's dad was deliberate and serious. When they'd split up, it had been traumatic and sad. As a permanent fixture in their home, Drake remembered what they were like in love with each other, had seen the stolen kisses and playful swats on the butt. He'd heard the declarations of love and the banter between them. Somewhere along the line, it had disappeared and been replaced with bitterness and resentment, arguments and manipulation.

Aside from the good times between Love's parents, Drake had never seen a thriving and happy relationship. The ones he'd seen had all ended with broken hearts. He'd figured it was because people expected things of their mates and when those expectations weren't met, the trust faltered. It was what scared him the most about being with Love.

Love was Drake's best friend, and he wanted her. He wanted her more than he'd ever wanted any woman before, more than he wanted to scrub in on a thrombectomy this afternoon. But that didn't necessarily mean he was willing to throw all his sensibilities out the window to risk winding up like Gloria and Dr. Leon, or his father and every single stepmother he'd had.

"Tell me the truth," Gloria said. "What's going on between you and my daughter?"

"We're trying to figure things out." Drake wasn't sure how much he wanted to tell his mother-in-law.

"I can ask you because I know you'll tell me the truth. Lovely likes to dismiss me, keep her life under wraps."

"You know your daughter. She's always been very private."

"This marriage—how did it happen?"

He shifted in his seat. "It just kind of did. I realized that my life was better with her in it and I popped the question." The lie rolled off his tongue so easily, it shocked him. But he went with it.

"I didn't hear you mention love. Do you love her?"

"I do." There was no confusion. Drake knew he loved his wife. Again, it still didn't mean they'd end up together. He'd rather be without her romantically than lose her altogether.

"I worry about her, ya know? I'm getting older, Drake. I want her to be settled already. She's so closed off to certain things. That's why I'm so grateful she has you, because you've opened her eyes to possibilities. You wade out in the deep end while she stays near the shallow end. Since she was a child, I've always tried to make her see the glory in living life on her own terms. I want her to stop and smell the snapdragons."

He barked out a laugh. "I think she'll be okay. She's driven, goal oriented."

"Like her father," Gloria mumbled, a hint of disgust in her voice.

"But I've seen her free, unbothered. She is your daughter, too."

Gloria smiled sadly. "I didn't want Love to be an only child."

This was news to him. "Really?"

"I miscarried three babies after God blessed me with Lovely. She's my little slice of heaven on earth. I'm so proud of her, and I know you'll take good care of her."

"Mom, you're scaring me. What's going on with you?"

She shrugged. "Nothing. Just thinking back on my life. It didn't work out with her father and me, but I never want her to give up on love."

Drake glanced at Gloria, took in her tired eyes. She was sick, possibly facing major surgery. Of course she'd be concerned about where her daughter would end up if she wasn't around. That was normal. But he hoped that time was many years away.

Chapter 13

Love opened the door and stepped in. "You called?"

Her father sat at his desk, pen in hand and a stack of files in front of him. She recalled how hard it was to be his daughter at times, and how she'd almost buckled from the pressure her first year of medical school.

It seemed like Love had had to fight for everything, including her medical school acceptance. Her father was old school. He believed in hard work and had refused to give her preferential treatment when it came to her admission to the program. She was expected to work twice as hard and get in on her own merits.

Love had tried to pretend that her father's refusal to help her in any way with school hadn't bothered her, but it had and still did. The man in front of her was well respected in the medical field, but all she'd ever wanted was his love and attention.

Rubbing the stubble on his chin, he gestured toward the chair in front of his desk. "Have a seat."

"I'll stand."

Dr. Leon, as everyone called him, used to be her hero and the most important man in her life. But that had changed somewhere around the time he'd left her mother and moved hundreds of miles away. He'd disappointed her time and time again, almost made it impossible to meet his lofty expectations. Yet she still hated to let him down.

"Why did you do it?" he asked after a few tense moments of silence.

"It seemed like the right thing to do at the time," she answered.

"Are you pregnant?"

"You already asked me that, and I told you no. I'm not sure why you're having such a hard time accepting my choice to marry Drake?"

"I've racked my brain over this, and I can't understand why you'd do this. Why would you throw your life away on a relationship that will never work?"

"You don't know that."

"Lovely, you're my daughter. I know you. You've wanted the big white wedding since you were a little girl. Yet you settle for a quick Las Vegas ceremony?"

"I know you're upset, but Drake is my husband. We're together, and I want to give this a chance. For once, why can't you support me?"

"Maybe I'm old-fashioned, but I expected any man that wanted to marry you to come to me first. You're my only child, Love. I would have liked the honor of giving you away."

"I'm sorry you weren't there, Daddy. I know Mom

wanted to be there, as well. But Drake didn't force me to marry him. He didn't do anything I didn't want him to do. Please understand that."

"I'm sorry, I don't understand it. And despite what you may think, I only want the best for you."

"If you can't see that Drake *is* what's best for me, I don't know what to tell you."

"Love, I just don't agree."

"Well, I'm glad it isn't your decision to make." She crossed her arms. "I mean, it's not like you don't know Drake, Daddy. He's the same person you took under your wing all those years ago. You taught him how to ride a bike, for Christ's sake. You were more like a father to him than his own."

"You're right. He is the same person I've known for years. Last I checked, Drake was looking for a career, not a wife. And that was just last month. He wants the high life, fly-in surgeries, penthouse view, guest lecturer. He wants fame and notoriety. You are fundamentally different people. This marriage will be over before it starts."

Love swallowed rapidly as her father ticked off the many reasons a relationship with Drake wouldn't work. She had to admit they were all reasons that ran through her mind daily. "You don't understand him. He would never hurt me."

"That's where you're wrong. I do understand. Mark my words, you'll end up heartbroken when he wakes up one morning and realizes he wants more."

It felt like a slap, and Love swayed on her feet. The words did more damage than she wanted to admit. The fact that her own father made it seem like she could never be enough for a man like Drake stung, but not more than the fact that she had wondered the same thing countless times over the past few weeks. Her father's words served only to heighten her own fears about their fate, especially since she'd fallen for Drake as hard and fast as he'd made love to her last night.

Frowning, she observed her father. A question had niggled at her mind for years. She'd never understood why her parents had divorced, and listening to her father just then, it all made sense. Clearing her throat, she asked, "Is that what happened with you and Mom?"

"This isn't about me and your mother."

"Isn't it? How else can you explain how mean you've been about this? I get it, though. You don't want me hurt. But Drake won't hurt me."

"He will," her father insisted. "You can't say what he won't do. Look, I like Drake. He's a talented doctor with a long career ahead of him."

"Then why are you punishing him at work?"

"I was angry, disappointed. I've remedied that as of today."

Love closed her eyes and sent up a silent "thank you, Lord."

"I respect him as a person," her father continued. "He's just not the man I want for my daughter."

"And Derrick is?"

"Lovely, he's a good man."

"He cheated on me. I can't believe you're pushing him on me, even knowing the truth."

"People make mistakes. But I know that Derrick is sorry for what he's done. He's honest about his shortcomings, humble. And I appreciate that about him."

Love shook her head, rolling her eyes at that ass-backward reasoning her father had thrown out. It pissed her off that the man who'd been larger than life to her at one point couldn't admit the real reason he was so against her marriage.

"Daddy, I wish you could see Drake the way I do." He opened his mouth to speak, but she forged ahead. "And I wish you'd stop making him like you, when that couldn't be further from reality. Yes, you hurt Mom. But that doesn't mean Drake will make the same choices. The fact that you expect my husband will treat me the way you treated my mother pisses me off. It not only insults my intelligence, but it hurts that you assume I'm not good enough to keep a man like Drake happy."

"Love, baby girl, that's not why—"

She nodded, praying the tears wouldn't fall. "It is, and it hurts. So, no, I won't take Derrick back. I'm married to Drake, and until you can respect that, we don't have anything else to say to one another."

Love stomped out of the office once again. She waited until she was on the other side of the closed door before she sagged against it, finally allowing the tears to fall. The only person breaking her heart at that moment was her father. She pulled her phone out of her pocket, tempted to call Drake. He was her safe place, after all.

Her phone rang before she could dial, though. Staring at the screen, at the familiar number, she decided to answer. "I'm glad you called. I need to see you."

Lunch at the hospital offered a wide variety of choices for a starving Love. She'd decided to go with something fattening after the argument she'd had with her father. With a plate of cheese fries and a juicy double cheeseburger, she headed toward the far right of the huge cafeteria, waving at a few friends on the way.

As she approached the table where he sat, Derrick was typing furiously on his phone. They'd eaten lunch at that table many times over the course of their relationship.

He smiled when he saw her, standing to greet her. Derrick placed a chaste kiss on her cheek and waited until she was settled before taking his seat again.

Eyeing her food, he chuckled. "Bad day?"

Love popped a fry in her mouth, moaning at the cheesy goodness. "You don't want to know the day I've had, Derrick."

"Try me."

"Daddy."

He nodded, seemingly understanding without a wordy explanation. "Another argument, huh?" He snatched a fry from her plate.

She shot him a sideways glance. "Can you say understatement?"

"Love, I'm sorry."

Her eyes flashed to his dark ones. "What are you sorry for?"

Derrick lifted his hands, then let them fall. "For hurting you, and then waltzing back into your life like you owed me something."

Love sat back, watching him as he explained that her father had tried to convince him to stick around and help drive a wedge between her and Drake. She was livid, had half a mind to send her father a "breakup" text, disowning him. He'd enlisted her ex to destroy her marriage. What nerve!

Derrick reached out, placed a hand on top of hers. "It's no secret that I don't care for Drake, but I respect your decision. I told your father that, as well."

Surprised, Love smiled, glad that she hadn't been completely wrong about Derrick. "Thank you."

"For what it's worth, I hope Drake can make you happy."

She flipped her hand over and squeezed his. "I know it's hard for you to say that, but I appreciate it. I wanted to see you because I felt like I had to be honest with you."

"I'm listening."

"Even if there was no Drake, I couldn't be with you." She felt his hand go slack in hers. "It's not to say I don't care for you, because I do, even after everything that's happened between us."

Love had a light-bulb moment as she sat across from the man she'd thought she'd spend the rest of her life with. As good as they were together, it wasn't enough for her. And Drake…even if they filed for divorce tomorrow, she'd never be the same. She'd been forever changed by this experience, and she was no longer willing to settle for less when she'd felt what true passion could be.

"I've changed," she admitted softly. "The person I am now is not willing to just accept everything someone gives her. I can admit that I played a huge part in the demise of our relationship, but I can't be with someone I don't trust. Long-distance relationships are hard, but I felt like you owed me more. And I just had to tell you that. I think you're a good man, but I'm not in love with you anymore. I hope you understand."

"Actually, I do. It's a hard pill to swallow, but you're right."

They sat for a minute in an awkward silence. Love wondered what he was thinking, but decided not to ask. They'd pretty much said it all, and she was ready to close the book on that chapter for good.

"So, are you going to eat those fries?" he asked.

She giggled and picked one up, pointing it at him. "Wouldn't you just love for me to say no."

"Seriously, I'm hungry."

They spent a few more minutes catching up, before he had to leave. He hugged her, and walked out of her life.

Drake watched his wife have lunch with her ex with narrowed eyes.

"Are you just going to let him worm his way back into her life?" Gloria said, elbowing him in the side.

He flinched, rubbing the spot she'd hit. "Damn, Mom. That hurt."

"Drake, that is your wife. You need to go over there and get your woman."

"They're just eating," he told her, more to convince himself than his pushy mother-in-law. "I can't keep making scenes at work. I told you about what happened the other day."

During their car ride that morning, Drake had confessed that he'd made a fool of himself at work and had since been tormented by his colleagues. His uncle-brother, El, had lead the charge, blazing on him every time he saw him. His younger brothers had also joined the group, making sure they mentioned his possessive ways every time they ran into him in the hall.

Drake noted the way Love laughed, and was entranced at the way her head fell back when she did so. She enjoyed Derrick's company, that much was clear. And he hated it. He hated him.

"Hey, I'm all for giving zero—"

"Shh," he hissed, before she finished her sentence with an f-bomb. Gloria and he had an understanding. There wasn't much he couldn't say to her, but he wanted to keep it clean.

"Hey," she repeated, placing a hand on her hip. "Don't shush me. You know I'm right."

"You're right," he grumbled reluctantly. "I'll talk to her later. Don't worry."

They watched as Derrick stood and hugged Love. Before Drake realized it, he'd stepped forward, halting in his tracks when Derrick rushed out of the cafeteria.

Gloria hooked her arm in his and pulled him toward Love, who was finishing her burger. "Hey, Lovely," she said, taking the empty seat across from her daughter and forcing him to take the seat beside her.

Love shot a glance at him. "Hey." She smiled at her mother. "Hi, Mom. How are you feeling today?"

"Better," Gloria said. "Especially now that Derrick is gone. I hope he's gone for good. Lovely, you really shouldn't be eating all that cheese. It will mess with your stomach."

As Gloria went on about cheese and the digestive system, Drake swept a hand up Love's leg and squeezed her thigh.

"Lovely Grace, are you listening to me?"

Drake chuckled, knowing that she had tuned her mother out.

"Sure," Love lied.

"I still want to throw you and Drake a reception."

Drake dug his fingers into Love's thigh. He'd spent the morning avoiding talk about a reception, but it seemed Gloria wouldn't be deterred.

"Mother, I don't think it's a good time," Love told her.

"I'm not going to deny that I was hurt when I found out about your hasty wedding. But I've moved past it. By the way, I heard you and Drake in the kitchen last night."

Drake choked and rubbed the back of his neck.

"Mother, please." Love covered her ears. "Oh, my God. I'm so embarrassed," she muttered.

"What? You know I have ears like a hawk," Gloria said innocently.

"Oh, God," Love grumbled. "Make it stop."

"Okay." Gloria folded a napkin into a little square, like she used to do when they were children. "Anyway, I had to look at myself in the mirror. I swore I'd never be as old-fashioned as my parents were. I didn't intend to raise my child the same way they raised me."

"Mother, you're nothing like your parents."

Drake knew the history. Love's grandparents had co-pastored one of those Southern Baptist churches in the backwoods of Tuscaloosa, Alabama, before moving to Las Vegas to start a ministry in what they called the den of sin. Her Nana and Papa didn't understand when Gloria showed up pregnant out of wedlock, and they disowned her. They hadn't even shown up for the wedding a few months before Love was born.

"So I can't be too mad you went and eloped without me or your father there," Gloria said. "But I can say I'm ecstatic that you married Drake. He's perfect for you. And in an effort to prove to you that I'm really okay with this decision, I want to give you two a reception."

"Mom, you have a lot going on right now."

"She's right, Mom," Drake agreed.

Gloria could need surgery, and he didn't want her stressing about something that didn't matter to him. He knew Love felt the same way.

"Can we table this discussion for after your appointment today?" Love picked up her mother's hand and kissed it. "I want us to focus on getting your health under control, right, Drake?"

"Exactly," he agreed. "If you want to help, fry me some chicken for dinner."

Love glanced over at Drake, who shrugged and ate one of her fries.

Gloria gave them a watery smile, stood and pulled them both into her arms. "I love you, my Lovely. You, too, Drake. You have made me so proud." She gave them each a kiss on the forehead before pulling back. "We have to go. I want to use the bathroom before my appointment."

As Gloria walked off ahead of them, Drake and Love followed at a good distance. He leaned into her. "I saw Derrick."

"You did," Love said, a sneaky smile on her plump lips. She was so ready to be kissed, and he wanted to push her into one of those little nooks and do it. But he'd promised himself he'd keep his hands to himself at work. It was becoming harder by the minute, though.

"Why was he here?"

She raised a brow. "Are you jealous?"

"Pretty much," he admitted.

She laughed, and his mouth went dry. "That was honest."

"I know no other way to be."

Nodding, she told him about her visit with her dad and the subsequent lunch with Derrick. "It was time to let him know, in no uncertain terms, that we are over."

Drake couldn't deny he was glad Love had handled Derrick, even though he still wanted to knock him out.

Love stopped in front of the restroom her mother had entered, and folded her arms over her chest. She grinned up at him, biting her lip. "I like that you're jealous."

He couldn't help it; he reached out and rubbed her bottom lip with his thumb. It took everything in him not to kiss her right then and there, gawkers be damned. "Well, I don't like when you laugh with other men."

She gasped. "You're hilarious. Am I supposed to be serious all the time, Drake?"

"When you're not with me."

She shoved him playfully, but he grabbed her wrist and pulled her to him. It was strange being like this with her in the hallway outside the cafeteria. Anybody could see them, but he didn't care. He imagined how she'd taste right then, could almost hear the breathless way she said his name when she was coming for him.

He leaned in closer, his hands tightening around her waist. His gaze lingered on her mouth, before he pressed his lips against hers. She pulled him against her, taking control of the kiss and prying his lips apart with her tongue. A low moan escaped from his throat.

Or was it hers? He honestly didn't know where he stopped and she began, they were so close.

Someone clearing a throat behind him put a halt to what was sure to escalate. He'd already spotted an empty nook to his left.

Love giggled against his mouth and they slowly backed away from each other. Gloria was standing with a hand on her hip. Around them, a few people clapped, and Drake took a bow.

"I'm going to go," he said, when the applause died down. He could still taste Love's lips, and fought back a groan. He hugged Gloria and placed a kiss on her forehead. "Bye, Mom." Then he turned to her daughter. Brushing her hair back, he whispered, "I'll see you later, Love."

She waved at him, and he saluted her, then left.

Chapter 14

Love tapped her foot against the tile as she replied to an email. Her mother sat on the exam bed, rambling on about how she was sick of doctors scheduling appointments for a certain time, then not even walking into the room until an hour later.

"Lovely?" she called. "Are you listening to me?"

Love gave her a grin. "I'm sorry, Mother. I had an urgent email. What were you saying?"

"Never mind." Gloria waved a dismissive hand. "You always do that—tune your poor mother out."

The fact was—and she was ashamed to admit it—she rarely listened to her mother completely. It was a big problem because her mom had a habit of sneaking things into the conversation when Love wasn't paying attention.

"Mom, I'm sorry. You have my undivided focus."

"I'm scared," Gloria whispered, tears welling in her eyes.

Shocked by the uncharacteristically emotional admission, Love scooted closer to the bed. Throughout her life, she had seen her mother loud, frantic, nosy, sweet, but never scared. She rubbed her knee. "Aw, Mom, it's going to be okay. No matter what, I'm going to take care of you."

It was the least she could do, because Gloria had always put her first.

Gloria dashed tears from her cheeks with both hands. "When your father left me, I tried my best not to let you see how devastated I was. I didn't want you to witness that and think all relationships were bad. I worried about you for so long. You'd be so wrapped up in school, and I wondered if you'd ever actually let yourself start to live. I wanted that for you so badly. I wanted you to be able to be free, because I wasn't."

Love found herself wiping her own eyes, as her mother continued, "To see you happy, and in love, makes me feel like I didn't fail you."

"Mom, please." Love leaned forward and embraced her. "You did not fail me. You've been there for me through everything. I don't know what I would have done without you." She held her gently as she cried into her shoulder. Love wasn't sure what was going on, but it frightened her.

"Lovely, I won't be around forever. It does my heart good to know that you will be well taken care of when I'm not here."

"Stop talking like that, Mom. I'm going to do whatever I have to do to make this okay, even if that means moving you to Michigan so that I can take care of you."

Gloria laughed. "Yeah, right. You'd hate living in the same house with me."

Love let out a shaky laugh of her own, grateful that her mother found anything funny. "I would, but I love you more than I love my solitude."

"Solitude? You have none of that now. Drake is there."

Love paused. Her mother was holding on to her marriage for dear life, it seemed. "True. It's been an adjustment."

"Don't be too hard on him."

Love smirked. She remembered when she'd refused to let Drake stay with her years ago when he'd been looking for a place to live. Now, he was living with her, sleeping with her. He had a toothbrush in her bathroom, underwear in her drawers.

What a difference a wedding and good sex made.

"I have a confession to make," Gloria whispered.

Curious, Love pulled back and met her gaze. "What is it?"

"When I first found out you and Drake were married, I thought you were up to something. I couldn't believe it. I even considered a drunken night might be the reason."

Love laughed. Loudly. "Wow, Mom. That's…something."

"I know. But watching you two together made me realize that you really do care for each other. You're in love."

Love thought about that for a moment. She did love Drake—really loved him. Not just because he was

Drake but because he was *her* Drake. Her husband. And she wanted it to stay that way.

It was hours later when Love got back to work. She opened the door to exam room three and stepped in to see her favorite patient. "Hi, Sydney."

Sydney Smith, her friend Jared's twin sister, looked up from a magazine and smiled. "Dr. Love."

They hugged. Normally, Love wouldn't do that with a patient, but Sydney had become a friend. The two had clicked immediately when Love had had the pleasure of delivering baby Brynn.

There was nothing more rewarding than being in the delivery room. Love enjoyed helping mothers bring babies into the world. Early on, she'd vowed to help women with conception problems and little or no access to health care realize the dream of having a child. It was her passion, and her ultimate goal was to open a specialist clinic devoted to women's health.

"What brings you in, Syd?" Love asked, taking a seat on the stool. She quickly docked her tablet and signed in to the system.

Syd sighed, her hazel eyes flashing. "I think Brynn is going to have a little brother or sister."

Love gasped. "What? So soon?"

Syd's little one was only two years old, and it had been a rough pregnancy. She'd ended up on bed rest for two months leading up to the harrowing birth of her daughter.

"Is Morgan ecstatic?"

Morgan and Sydney had an adorable, devoted relationship. There was no hiding the love they had for each other. Love had been honored to attend the wedding, right there in the hospital chapel. Love recalled the despair in Syd's eyes the day they'd brought him in with a life threatening gunshot wound, after an attempted robbery. It had been touch and go, but Morgan eventually pulled through and popped the question a few minutes after he'd regained consciousness.

Ironically, Drake had been a first year surgical resident in the OR during Morgan's surgery. The two men had become cool after that, often meeting for basketball at the gym during the week.

Syd crossed her legs, her wedding band sparkling under the lights. "Girl, you know he is, but I'm not so sure I'm ready to go through another pregnancy. It was hard, and I was miserable."

Love laughed, and typed a few notes into her tablet. "Are you concerned about being able to carry to term again?"

It was a common fear for women who'd had difficult pregnancies.

Syd bit her lip. "It's crossed my mind. I don't want to spend my entire pregnancy worried. Then, too, my business is booming. We just expanded our current building, and we're scouting spots in Canton. It might not be the best time to have a baby. Brynn is a handful already."

Love nodded. Syd owned the Ice Box, a restaurant in the neighboring town of Ypsilanti. The city was named in honor of Demetrius Ypsilanti, a Greek revolutionary leader, and was the home of Eastern Michigan University. Love spent a lot of time in Ypsilanti, whether she was eating at one of the many restaurants in Depot Town or hanging out at Sydney's bar with Drake.

"I understand," Love assured her. "But let's start with a pregnancy test. There's no point in worrying yet. You don't know if you're going to have a bad pregnancy, so we can't make assumptions."

Syd sighed. "Right. Let's do it."

Love pulled up Syd's medical records and skimmed them. "I want you to head down and get your blood drawn right after your appointment. I won't do an ultrasound or anything until we get a positive test."

"Thanks, Love."

Love prepared a lab requisition and wrote a script for prenatal vitamins. "Anything else going on?"

"Nothing much. How are things going with you? Last time I saw you at the bar, you were drowning your sorrows with your best friend."

Love snorted. "That was a while ago."

"It was. He's a hottie, by the way."

Grinning, Love tugged at her ear. "We got married a few weeks ago."

"Are you serious?"

"Yes. It wasn't planned. It just kind of happened."

"That's awesome, Love. Are you thinking of starting a family soon? Because I'm going to selfishly ask you to hold off until I have my baby."

Love barked out a laugh. "Girl, you don't have to worry about that."

"You never know. I mean, kids were the last thing on my mind when I started seeing Morgan. And then it just happened."

Love clicked on the calendar of her tablet. Her period wasn't due for another week or so, but Syd was right. Essentially, they'd done nothing to prevent a pregnancy. The few times she and Drake had had sex, they hadn't used a condom. Love was on birth control, yes, but she'd seen that fail time and time again.

Her hands trembled as she finished with her notes. The thought of being pregnant herself was enough to make her rethink everything. Making love to Drake was becoming one of her favorite things to do. So much so that she'd been counting down the hours until she could see him again. But they had to take better precautions, because neither of them was ready for a baby.

"Love?" Syd called.

Shaking herself out of her thoughts, she offered her a small smile. "Sorry. A lot going on right now." Not wanting to get into the details of her marriage, she explained about her mother instead. "My mom is in town dealing with some health issues."

Her mother's appointment with the surgeon had gone well. He'd determined that amputation should be a last resort. In the meantime, he set up Gloria on a new treatment he was hyped on. Gloria had sobbed openly at the news.

Love still wanted her mother to consider moving to Michigan, or at least staying for an extended visit. But Gloria was stubborn, and hadn't budged.

"We should really catch up over drinks soon," Love told Sydney. "Well, I can drink and you can have apple juice and pretend it's cognac."

They both laughed then.

Syd stood up and took the form from Love's outstretched hand. "Thanks. I'm going to head to the lab and then go to work. Please let me know as soon as you get the results."

"I certainly will."

The two said goodbye and Love started toward the office. Along the way she pulled out her phone and typed a text to Drake: What if I'm pregnant?

Drake stumbled and almost took an L in the middle of the floor. His *wife* had sent him a text asking what would happen if she were pregnant. Hell, the thought was enough to send him straight to the bar. But he was scheduled to scrub in on a surgery in a few hours and wanted to study a bit beforehand. Dr. Leon had sent him a curt email reminding him of his obligation to the hospital, informing him that his recent change in marital status would not grant him any favors, and letting him know that he'd be assisting him with a heart transplant.

Drake had hoped to talk to Dr. Leon again, but it was obvious the older man didn't want much to do with him outside of work. He suspected the recent change of heart had more to do with his father's demands than anything else, which pissed Drake off. But at least he knew where he stood with his mentor now.

He stared at the text, dissecting the words. *What if I'm pregnant?* Drake was hit with a dilemma. Should he go to her and ask her what she meant, or send a lighthearted text like "stop playing around. LOL."

Deciding against both options, he typed: We'll talk later. He hesitated for a minute, deleting and retyping the same message at least three times. Sighing, he hit Send and dropped his phone into his pocket.

A few minutes later, he was knocking on El's office door.

El swung the door open, a pinched look on his face.

"You do know that I actually have a job that I do on a daily basis."

Pushing past his uncle-brother, he made himself comfortable on a little bench by the window. "We need to talk."

"You're lucky my appointment canceled." El took his seat, crossing one ankle over his knee. "What do you want?"

"Love might be pregnant."

El stared at him, a blank expression on his face.

"Say something," Drake said. "Wait." He pulled a dollar out of his lab coat and slapped it on the desk.

El shook his head. "In a minute, I'm going to recommend you spend a few days in the ward. Take that damn dollar back." He picked the bill up and flung it at Drake.

The weightless paper didn't make it far, landing on the floor in front of the desk. "Keep it. I need to know you won't tell anyone about this."

"I'm a little insulted that you feel the need to constantly swear me to secrecy, as if I make a habit of telling your business."

El the psychiatrist would never even think of sharing a patient's stories with anyone. El the uncle-brother would definitely spill the beans at the wrong moment, like a family barbecue or something. Of course, he wouldn't do it maliciously. It was just what "big brothers" did. El had tormented him and his younger siblings for years. If that meant embarrassing them in front of everyone and their mama, El couldn't resist at times.

Drake jumped to his feet, pacing the room with long, impatient strides. "We haven't talked about a divorce," he confessed. "It's kind of an afterthought. When we left Vegas, we were committed to ending this marriage as soon as possible. And we haven't even hired a lawyer. What does that mean?"

What Drake didn't add was that he wasn't as miserable as he'd imagined he would be. Being married to Love wasn't awful. It was actually pretty damn good. "It's only been a few weeks, but it feels right to me, like this is the way it's supposed to be between us."

"You slept with her again," El said. It wasn't a question.

Drake glared at him. "How the hell do you do that?"

"Occupational hazard."

"More than once." Drake pinched his nose, feeling overheated. "I'm not sure I can stop at this point."

"Are you in love with her?"

It was unrealistic, plain and simple. They'd been married for only a few weeks, had never even been on a real date. But he was sure he was. Hell, he'd probably always been a little bit in love with her. "It's impossible, right?"

El shrugged. "Not really. Not with your history with Love."

"I guess not, but it's still weird." The feeling only seemed to intensify as the days passed.

"Love is a beautiful person, bruh."

Drake smiled to himself, thinking about his wife. Love was beautiful and intelligent, and she took good care of him. She was the best of both worlds. "What happens if this doesn't work out?"

He didn't expect a verbal answer. It was El's style to just let him talk until he figured it out himself. So when his brother said, "Why would you go into this thinking it will fail?"

Sighing, Drake told El about the confrontation with Love's father. "The man has a point. I suck at being committed to any woman. If I mess this up, I not only lose my job, but I will destroy the best relationship I've ever had. She's my best friend, my confidante, my support. Do I risk that for an uncertain outcome?"

"I think your question should be, how can you not? Look, love isn't easy. You know that. It hurts, but when it's good, it's really good."

Drake knew El was speaking from experience. Even though things hadn't worked out with El and Avery, his uncle-brother still believed that love was worth it. "You're right."

"Are you afraid to fail, afraid to take a chance on Love?"

"It's not like I had a good role model on being faithful and committed to one woman." Drake had made it a point to date wide and far. His father had set the example for him. But El's assertion that he was afraid to take a chance on Love was wrong. One thing that Drake always did was bet on Love. She'd never failed him. That alone made him want to be what she needed, whether it was with her or without her.

"I don't want to disappoint her. If I hurt her, I hurt me."

"Don't you think Love knows that about you?"

He didn't even blink before answering, "Yes. She knows everything about me."

"And she loves you, anyway."

That she did. Drake bent down, picked up the dollar bill and dropped it on El's desk. "You earned that today."

"Get the hell out of here."

Drake barked out a laugh. "I do have to study. I better get to it."

"Wait, all this mushy talk, and I conveniently forgot to ask about this whole pregnancy thing."

Drake told El about Love's text, and his uncle-brother snorted in amusement. "Wow, you two are made for each other. I'm assuming Love is on some sort of birth control, correct?"

Pausing, Drake thought about that for a moment. They'd never talked about it, but knowing her, she had it under control. He nodded. "I guess. I can't see her not being on the pill or something."

"Well, I suggest you definitely have that conversation. Can't have any Drake Juniors running around the hospital."

"Shut up." The thought of a mini-Drake or a little Lovely was uncomfortable, but a pregnant and glowing Love was appealing on some level.

"Hey, I'm just saying…"

"I gotta go. Basketball tomorrow?"

"Sure thing. Are you going to that fund-raiser next week?"

Drake groaned, unable to hide his disgust. "I am, unfortunately."

"Tell me about it. I won't be there long, though. One of my patients will need me."

Drake waved a dismissive hand. "And you know that already?"

"Yep."

Drake snatched his dollar from the table. "I need

this back to buy a bag a chips out of the vending machine."

Drake made plans to meet El for breakfast in the morning, before heading to the gym. Then, he gathered his things and went to see his wife. They had to talk.

Chapter 15

Love sat on a swing in the park next to her condo rental, a beer in hand. The day had been longer than she'd hoped, and she'd needed a breath of fresh air and solitude. It was cold as hell, but she was bundled up. And she wasn't pregnant. Thank God.

She peered up at the endless sky. The chill of the night was somehow overshadowed by the magnificence of the stars. One of her favorite things to do was visit the planetarium. Love was a proud nerd. Astronomy was one of her favorite subjects in school, and she'd spent hours at the College of Southern Nevada Planetarium as a young girl. Even now, as an adult, she would walk over to the University of Michigan Museum of Natural History and sit in the planetarium. Nothing beat the real thing, though. And the clear night above her was proof that God existed.

Drake pulled into his parking spot, and she watched him hop out of the car and grab his things. He was so confident in everything he did, from school to work to driving. They hadn't talked much since she'd sent the dreaded text earlier. His three-word response only served to ramp up her anxiety about their situation.

She could admit that she wasn't as experienced as he was with the opposite sex. While she hated to think of him with other women, even before he was with her, she knew he'd had many lovers. She'd had only three: terrible sex with the popular jock in high school, Derrick, and now Drake. Bad-sex guy had ruined her first time by behaving like a jerk during and after. She wasn't even sure why she'd done it. She didn't even like the guy that much.

Love took another swig of her beer and tugged her favorite Michigan hat over her ears. Drake had given it to her for her birthday a few years earlier. He'd had it specially made for her. It was blue, with hashtag "Hail" in gold writing across the front. It was a University of Michigan thing, short for "Hail to the Victors," the Michigan Fight Song.

Drake spotted her on his way into the building and headed over to her. "What's up?" he asked. "You do know it's forty degrees outside."

She smiled at him. "I'm bundled up."

"Did you bring an extra?" he asked, gesturing to her beer.

Pulling one out of her coat pocket, she handed it to him. "Of course."

He set his stuff down, and sat in the swing next to her. "Long day."

"Tell me about it."

They swayed in their swings for several minutes, in a comfortable silence. Drake broke the ice first when he said, "You're not pregnant, Love."

Giggling, she finished off her beer. "I know."

He glanced over at her, sending a bolt of awareness through her body. "What was that about?"

She toed the dirt below her and hooked her arms around the swing chains. "I guess I panicked. Sydney came into the hospital, thinking that she was pregnant." The results of Syd's test had already come back positive. Love had called her friend personally to deliver the news.

"Good. I'm sure Morgan is happy."

Syd had cried uncontrollably on the phone after she gave her the results. Initially, Love didn't know how to react, whether they were tears of joy or not. Eventually, after the tears subsided, Syd exclaimed that she was happy and couldn't wait to meet her new bundle of joy.

"He is," Love told him. "The whole situation got me thinking. We haven't really discussed sex. We just keep having it."

Drake laughed then, a low, husky chuckle. "Actually, I don't think we've had enough," he said with a wink.

Love pushed him away from her. "Ha ha. I'm trying to be serious here."

He tapped his beer bottle against his thigh. "Fine. I'm being serious with you."

She twisted in the swing until she was facing him. "You should know that I am on birth control."

"I figured you were."

Love had thought about how to broach the subject

of the marriage and what they were ultimately going to do about it. But the selfish part of her wanted to enjoy him for a little while longer, before they had to start thinking about lawyers and court dates.

"Do you think we're past the point of no return?"

His eyes flashed to hers, locked on them. Love sucked in a deep breath, waiting for him to say something. Words didn't come, though. Only silence, for what seemed like an eternity. She wanted to look away, but couldn't force herself to break the trance.

"Drake," she finally croaked, clutching her throat. "Are we—"

Before she could finish her sentence, he grabbed the plastic-coated chain of her swing, pulled her to him and took her lips in a searing kiss. She gripped the chains, held on for dear life as he kissed her hard, parting her lips with his tongue.

He broke the kiss first, leaned his forehead against her shoulder. "Love, I want to be honest with you. At this point, I'm not sure I want to let this go."

Her heart soared at his admission. She'd been thinking the same thing. The more time she spent with him, the more she wanted to spend with him. Thoughts of late dinners, weekend getaways, Top of the Park in the summer, with her resting between his legs while they watched a movie on the big screen… she envisioned it all in her mind. She found herself thinking about him, even when she should have been studying or listening at lectures. It had been only a few weeks, but he'd branded her.

"I'm glad you said that," she said. "I feel the same way."

He closed his eyes, letting out a heavy sigh. "Good."

"Good."

Drake stood up and tossed their empty bottles into a nearby recycling bin. He walked over to her, ran the back of his finger over the tip of her nose. "You're cold. Let's go in. I'll warm you up."

"Not yet. We have to race."

He grinned. "You're silly. We may have done that when we were kids, but I'm too old for that now."

"You act like you're ready for Geritol. Sit down."

"Okay." He sat on the swing. "Ready, set, go."

Just as she did when she was a kid, Love pumped her legs, propelling the swing higher. The brisk air against her cheeks and the sheer happiness she felt from doing something so simple and free with Drake made her feel giddy. As their swings moved higher, she screamed with glee. He was going to beat her to the top, as he always did, but her dismount would clinch the score.

"You ready?" he asked, from way above her.

"Go ahead."

Without warning, he jumped, soaring through the air to land on the dirt. He stumbled, but remained standing.

"Yes, you suck," she teased.

"Just jump, woman."

At the apex of her next swing Love kicked forward, flying up, then down. When she hit the ground, it was a perfectly stuck landing. She did a fist pump and took a bow. "Yay! I still got it."

Catching her breath, she beamed up at him. He

rubbed her shoulders. "I can admit when I fall short. You did good, baby."

She wasn't sure when she'd started being his "baby," but she'd take the endearment gladly. She rose up on the tips of her toes and brushed her lips against his. "Race you home," she murmured against his mouth before taking off.

Drake turned off the lights in the kitchen and started up the stairs. They'd spent the evening watching a movie with Gloria and eating popcorn. Since Gloria had insisted they all spend "family" time together, Drake hadn't had a chance to cozy up with Love the way he wanted. It was his turn now.

Opening the bedroom door, he halted at the sight of his *wife* standing before him in nothing but a pair of thin lacy panties.

"Drake!" She folded her arms over her bare chest, covering herself. "You should really knock."

"It's too late for shyness, Love. I've seen everything." He burst out in a laugh, tugging his shirt over his head, then set his watch on the nightstand.

A pillow against the back of his head knocked him forward. He rounded on her, picking up a throw pillow and tossing it at her. She ducked easily and ran to the other side of the bed. They stood facing each other, her chest heaving as her eyes shone. Love picked up another pillow, raised it above her head and swung it at him. He grabbed it and pulled, but she didn't give up easily.

"Let go!" she ordered.

"Don't hit me," he warned.

She eyed him, her grip tight on the pillow. "Let go."

"You let go."

It was a battle of wills, and she had the upper hand. Only because she was basically naked. Her smooth brown skin was waiting to be touched, caressed... kissed.

"Come here," she demanded, with hooded eyes.

He released his hold on the pillow and circled the bed. Hooking a finger into the waistband of her panties, he tugged her forward. Sweeping his hand over her chest, then her shoulders, he watched her eyes darken with desire for him. The control he had over her in the bedroom was like a drug. There would never be a better high. The more she gave him, the more he wanted.

Before he could kiss her, though, she smacked him in the head with that damn pillow and bolted toward the master bathroom. He jumped on top of the bed and caught her, wrapping his arms around her waist, and pulled her against him.

Laughing, Love told him to put her down. She snorted, gasping for air as he spun her around and dropped her on the bed.

Love rolled over on her back, fanning herself. She pointed at him. "The look on your face..." She dissolved into a fit of laughter again.

He climbed over her, between her legs. Grabbing both her thighs, he yanked her forward until he was pressed against her heat.

He trailed kisses down her neck until he reached her breast, pulling her nipple into his mouth and sucking until she cried out his name.

She tugged at his hair, urging him up and kissing

him with an urgency. He pulled back first, smirking when she cursed in frustration.

A pretty pout formed on her lips. "You're playing with my emotions."

"Are you ready?"

Love nodded, and her tongue darted out to moisten her lips. Drake mimicked her action, running his tongue over her full mouth before he kissed her. He groaned into her mouth when she rubbed him through his pants.

"You have on too many clothes," she mumbled.

She helped him unbutton his pants, and he kicked them and his underwear off at the same time. Settling between her legs, he placed a soft kiss on her lips and pushed inside her. He held still, relishing the feel of her. It was too intense, almost too much.

"You're so beautiful," he whispered.

She grinned. "You are, too."

Drake kissed her forehead, her cheeks, then her chin and finally her mouth. "I love you."

The words left his mouth before he could stop them. His pulse raced as he wondered if he should backtrack. Had he ruined the moment?

She arched her hips against him, taking him in farther. He stifled a groan, tried to hold it together.

"I love you, too."

A whimper escaped as he moved, slowly at first, taking his time to work her into a frenzy. She squirmed beneath him, writhing as the thrusts grew more intense. He was ready to let go, but he needed her with him.

Gripping her hips, he flipped over on his back. She sat astride him, her hands planted on his chest and her hips grinding down on him. He sat up, smoothed a hand up her back. She wrapped her arms around his neck, and they rocked together, giving themselves over to each other.

"Let go," he said, guiding her movements.

Slick with sweat, they picked up the pace. Her fingernails scraped his back, and he bit down on her shoulder. She groaned, long and hard, as her orgasm ripped through her. He felt his release build, then he exploded with her name on his lips.

Later, they sat facing each other, her legs flung over his. Moaning, she said, "This is so good."

"Want more?" he asked.

"Yes, please."

He fed her another spoonful of banana pudding. After they'd made love a third time, she'd told him she wanted something sweet to eat. He'd sneaked down to the kitchen, careful not to make too much noise and wake up Gloria, and pulled out everything he could find. In the bed with them was a bowl of banana pudding, a slice of lemon pound cake, a brownie and Jell-O. He broke off a piece of cake and popped it into his mouth.

"How is it?" Love asked.

Drake scowled. It wasn't the best cake he'd ever tasted, but he liked to support entrepreneurs. One of the patient techs had ideas to start a cottage industry baking cakes and wanted him to be her taster. "Not good."

Love wrinkled her nose. "I told you to stop buying food from those people at the hospital. You never know what their houses look like. They could have bugs." She shook her head. "Yuck."

"I'll try anything once." He squeezed her thigh, leaned in and kissed her. She caressed his face as they deepened the kiss.

When she pulled back and dipped her spoon in the red Jell-O, he took a minute to look at her. She was a vision, with her hair wild and free. His oversize shirt hung off her shoulders, exposing her bare skin.

They ate in silence, devouring the food in front of them. Finished, she fell against the mattress. "Woo, that was yummy."

He set their dishes on the bedside table and lay back next to her. They stared at the ceiling, seemingly in their own thoughts.

"Drake?" she asked, rising up on her elbow and looking down at him.

"Hmm?"

"Did we just declare our love for each other?"

Chuckling, he confirmed that they had in fact done that. "I meant what I said."

"Why do you love me?"

He shook his head. Leave it to Love to ask the hard questions. "I've loved you since I was two years old."

"Drake, that doesn't count. We were in Pull-Ups."

"It counts, because I feel like you being my best friend has contributed to the way I love you now."

"How so?"

"I loved you before we were us, and I love you more now *because* we're us."

"Aw, you're so sweet. And corny." She laughed.

"I'm glad I can still make you laugh."

She wrapped her arms around his waist and snuggled into him. "What do we do now?"

From his experience with Love, he knew he had to

let her set the pace. He knew what he wanted, and he didn't second-guess it. They were taking a big leap, but he was ready to jump, as long as she was with him. The easy way they were with each other confirmed that they could make it work. The awkwardness of the morning after their wedding had disappeared. Love was comfortable with him, invested in them.

"We take it day by day," he said. "Are you good with that?"

She pressed her cheek against his chest, kissed him right above his heart. "Yes, I am."

He heard the growl of her stomach. "Are you still hungry?"

"Oh, my God, that is so embarrassing, and so not sexy."

"I can try to cook you something."

"I want to live to see tomorrow." She giggled. "I have a taste for fish and grits, but it's too late to eat. I'm already going to pay for this dessert break."

"Aw, shoot. I must have put it down if you're talking about making my favorite meal."

She pinched him. "Shut up. Go to sleep. I'll make you fish and grits tomorrow."

The room descended into silence again. He squeezed her tight. "Good night. I love you."

"Love you, too."

Chapter 16

The Cadillac Club, an exclusive society, hosted a fund-raiser for the hospital every spring. Each year they awarded countless scholarships to prospective college students at the Annual Beau/Debutante Ball for high school seniors of color. They were also what Love considered a black elite social group.

Ann Arbor had a large population of affluent African Americans—doctors, lawyers, business owners and executives in local companies. True, they donated money to countless charities, but in doing so, some of them looked down on the people they were trying to help.

The Jackson family—more specifically, Drake's grandfather—was a founding member of the club. They were honoring his father with an award for philanthropy, and Love had promised Drake she'd be at the gala—even though she hated events like these.

Formal dinners were not her idea of fun, especially when it was an event that served one main purpose: to provide affluent individuals with a venue to act superior to other people. Love preferred low-key events. She'd rather be chilling in a bar with a bowl of peanuts and a big screen TV than attending a tense, stuffy dinner.

As she and Drake walked into the ballroom, his hand on the small of her back, she felt extremely uncomfortable. It had been a week since they'd declared their love for each other, and things were good. But they hadn't yet been around Drake's father together.

They'd spent the last week in a little bubble, holed up in bed or sneaking off at work to have lunch together or make out in the residents' lounge.

Love shifted, pulled at her gown. "I do not want to be here," she grumbled.

"We won't stay long," Drake whispered against her ear. "You look beautiful, though."

He'd told her that countless times already that evening. And she felt beautiful. Dr. Law had sent a limousine to pick them up, because heaven forbid one of his sons show up in a car. She'd been on edge for the whole ride, until Drake made her come so hard in the back of the limo she couldn't think about anything but him.

Sighing, she asked, "Promise?"

"I'm counting down the minutes till we leave."

The ballroom was gorgeous. The dusty rose and champagne color scheme was elegant and timeless. It was obvious the club had spared no expense to ensure everyone enjoyed the party and would be talking about it for months. Waiters walked around with trays of champagne, floral arrangements graced each tabletop, silver gleamed in the chandelier lighting. Everything seemed to sparkle. Love was impressed.

"Hey, bruh." Drake's younger brother Ian, one of the twins, approached them. The two men embraced and Ian gave Love a kiss on the cheek. "Hello, sister-in-law."

Love winked at him. He was like a little brother to her, too. "Hi, brother-in-law. You look good."

"And if you weren't married to my brother, I might have to take you home for the night."

"Watch it," Drake warned.

"Hey, I call it like I see it, and your wife is wearing some dress."

Love thanked Ian for the compliment. It had taken her hours to get ready. She hadn't been able to decide on what to wear. She'd purchased two gowns because she'd been torn. In the end, she'd chosen the black one. Nude mesh fabric with beaded accents created an illusion of a sheer back and side panels. It fitted her like a glove. Her hair was swept to the side in a delicate updo. From the moment he saw her, Drake hadn't been able to keep his eyes off her.

"Dad was looking for you," Ian murmured to Drake. "He was ready to send me out to fetch you."

Drake shrugged. "He knew I was coming. Where's Myles?"

Ian shrugged in turn. "Hell if I know. Probably working."

Myles was Ian's twin brother, but the two could not be more different. Ian was carefree, while Myles was closed off, serious. Of all the siblings, Myles was the most like Dr. Law. The twins were only seven months younger than Drake. Dr. Law had had two women pregnant at the same time.

Ian was dressed in a charcoal gray tuxedo, his short hair and beard groomed. He and Drake were around the same height, while Myles was a little shorter. Love took a moment to admire her husband in his black tuxedo. She loved a man in a suit and Drake wore one well. Love hadn't encountered a Jackson man that wasn't fine. Even Dr. Law was a devastatingly handsome man.

Ian nursed a tumbler filled with an amber-colored liquor. She suspected it was scotch. That was his drink of choice. "I was subjected to lecture two million ten about how he has high expectations for my career, and I should stop volunteering and focus on school," Drake's brother said drily.

Ian spent time volunteering with the Red Cross. Love had worked with him on several projects, and she appreciated his heart for service. Dr. Law could learn a thing or two from his sons.

"Where is Melanie?" Drake asked.

"She's out of town," Ian said. "Claimed she had to attend a conference in Seattle. I think she's full of it."

Melanie, or Mel, was the youngest of the Jackson brood. She was happily enjoying her college years, partying and traveling without a care in the world.

"Aw, I was hoping to see her," Love said.

"Hello, family." Myles, with his hands stuffed in the pockets of his heather-gray tuxedo, stepped up to them. He kissed Love on the cheek and shook Drake's hand. "I see the gang is all here."

"I'm glad you finally left the hospital," Love told him. Myles stayed at the hospital more than required. "It's time you live your life."

"Congratulations on the wedding," he replied, changing the subject. "I'm shocked. All these years, and you just up and decide to get married. I don't get it."

"You sound like Dad," Ian said. "I'm glad you did it, Drake. You got a good woman."

Drake wrapped an arm around her waist, pulled her closer and placed a kiss to her temple. "I know. You don't have to tell me."

"Well, if it isn't my boys," Dr. Law said as he approached. "And my new daughter-in-law." He greeted his sons with handshakes and gave her a hug. "Good to see you, Lovely."

She smiled. "Same to you."

Love couldn't help but feel some type of way about Dr. Law after hearing about how he'd lied to Drake about his mother for all those years. She wanted to give him a piece of her mind. One day, she'd get her chance.

"Drake, I have some colleagues I need you to meet."

Love smiled when Drake shot her a look as he followed his father away. She scanned the ballroom and spotted her own dad on the other side of the room. She'd expected him to be there. He was a member of the club, although not as prominent as Dr. Law.

Love walked over to the bar and ordered a club

soda. She wasn't in the mood for alcohol. She had an early shift in the morning.

"Hello, Lovely," her father said. "I was wondering if you were going to try and avoid me tonight."

She turned to him. "Hello, Dad."

He hugged her. "You're beautiful."

"Thank you."

"Where's your husband?"

Love didn't miss the sarcasm. Her father was still salty with her and Drake for getting married. "He's with his father. Dad, I really need this to stop. I hate fighting with you."

He let out a heavy sigh. "I'm sorry."

"Are you?"

"I am. I shouldn't have said or done the things I did. You're my daughter, and I love you. I just want you to be happy. Can you forgive me?"

Love eyed him. "Can you promise to leave Drake alone?"

There was a long silence, and Love wondered what he was going to say next. Was this an act?

"I promise."

She hugged her father, shutting her eyes when his arms closed around her. A hug from Dr. Leon Washington was a rare thing, and she savored it. "Thank you, Dad."

Drake stood on the far side of the ballroom, a letter from Johns Hopkins in hand. They'd accepted him into their cardiothoracic surgery residency program. It was a fellowship that he'd applied for last year, before Love.

Two months earlier he wouldn't have hesitated. But now...

"What are you going to do?" his father asked.

Drake's dad had given a lecture at Johns Hopkins and run into the chief of surgery while there. The two were old friends, and the other doctor had given him the letter to hand deliver to Drake.

Scratching his forehead, Drake shook his head. "I don't know."

"You've worked for this."

Drake was skeptical about his father's sudden show of support. He could see right through him. This was about Love, plain and simple. "I'm married, Dad. I can't just up and leave. I can continue here."

"Son, this is a huge opportunity. You can't pass something like this up."

"Don't tell me what I can or can't do. All of a sudden you're concerned? I wonder why I find that hard to believe."

He caught a glimpse of Love walking toward them, and tucked the letter in his inside jacket pocket.

"Hey, babe," she said.

Drake hugged her, kissing her brow. "Hey."

He couldn't stop looking at Love. Her beauty glowed from within. When he'd first seen her dressed and made up earlier, he couldn't breathe. It overwhelmed him at times, the way he loved her. The thought of leaving her made him sick.

"I spoke with my dad," she said.

He glanced at his own father. "I'll talk to you soon." He led Love away without another word to him. "How did that go?" he asked her.

"It went well. He apologized."

"That's good."

She eyed him curiously. "Are you okay?"

Drake wasn't sure if he should tell Love about the acceptance letter, especially since they'd decided to try and make their relationship work. But he'd never lied to her before, not about anything serious. Sure, he'd told her on a number of occasions he hadn't eaten her food, but this was big. Taking that fellowship would put them in different states for three years. Even if they did decide to try and make it work long-distance, the odds of them succeeding were low.

"I'm fine, just irritated with my dad," he told her. It wasn't an outright lie, just not the entire truth. "Let's take our seats. Dinner will start soon."

Drake and Love joined Ian and Myles at a table. His father was seated at the adjacent table with his current wife.

"What do you have a taste for?" Drake asked Love, frowning at the menu card in front of him. He hated these highbrow events. The food always consisted of rubbery chicken, overcooked beef or dry fish.

She hummed. "Um… I'm thinking the chicken dish. What about you?"

"The rib eye."

"Okay, get your steak and we can share my chicken. I have to save room for my cheesecake."

Drake nodded, distracted by the skin peeking out through the slit in her dress. He reached out and brushed a hand over her knee. "I want to take you home."

"Yeah? I want you to take me home. But we have to stay, at least until your father gets his award."

"Drake?"

He turned at the sound of his name being called. Howard and Dawn Harris approached the table. Though the couple were colleagues of his, he couldn't stand either one of them. They were nothing but trouble, and had caused many problems at work.

"Is that you, Love?" Dawn said in a saccharine tone.

Love smiled brightly at them. "Yes, it's me."

"You clean up nice," Dawn said.

Love tapped a finger on the table. Drake knew she couldn't stand Dawn, either. "How are you two?" she asked.

Drake picked up his glass of cognac and raised it in greeting. "Hi, Dawn. Howard," he said drily.

"We're good," Dawn replied. "I didn't know you'd be here."

"Why not?" Drake asked. "My father is winning the award of distinction."

"I heard that you two are seeing each other now." The other woman folded her arms over her chest.

"We're married," he said. "Happily. But you know that, right? You've been the one spreading rumors about us around the hospital."

Love's eyes widened, but she played along. "Which is surprising to us because you don't know anything about our relationship."

Dawn's cheeks turned red and she nervously clutched her purse strap. "Who said I did that? I rarely even think about you."

Love piped up, "Oh, how wonderful. I don't think about you, either."

Without another word, Dawn pulled Howard away in a huff.

Drake smiled at Love. "You're brilliant."

She looked at him, her eyes sparkling in the dim lighting. "Well, you married me. I guess that makes you brilliant, too."

Chapter 17

Love looked up when Drake walked into the bedroom. "Hey," she said, setting her pen down on her book. "You're home earlier than I thought."

"Yeah, I'm tired." He undressed, then slipped on his pajamas.

He sat on the edge of the bed, bowed his head. She crawled toward him and hugged him from behind, pressing her lips to his cheek. "Do you need anything? I made dinner."

Drake kissed her hand, held it against his mouth. "You are too good to me. I don't deserve you."

"Yes, you do. We deserve each other." She brushed her lips against his. "I can warm up some food for you."

Some women hated the thought of taking care of their men, but Love embraced it. She loved cooking for Drake, and making sure that he was eating well. It was relaxing to her, and not that different from how she'd been with him before everything changed.

He shook his head. "No, I'm good. I ate at the hospital."

It wasn't like Drake to turn down food. Especially food she made. He loved her cooking. It had been a busy week for them, and they'd barely seen each other. All week Drake had been acting distant, too. She couldn't figure out why, though. Part of her worried that he'd reconsidered everything. When she'd asked him, he told her he was just tired. She'd known him long enough to know when he wasn't being entirely truthful, which concerned her, because he'd never lied to her before.

"Are you sure you're okay?"

"I'm fine, Love." He stood up. "I'm going to take a shower."

The next morning, Love woke up to an empty bed. Drake had withdrawn the night before and it really concerned her.

She walked downstairs, hoping to find him in the kitchen or the living room. No Drake. Just then, she heard the front door open.

Drake rushed in with a cup of coffee. When he spotted her, he shot her a stiff smile.

"Hey," he said, dropping his keys on the table. "What are you doing up so early?"

Love shrugged. "I was looking for you. Where'd you go?"

"I went to the hospital to check on a patient."

Love couldn't tell if he was lying about the patient,

but something was definitely wrong. "Do you have to go back?"

"Not for a couple hours. I came back to get some sleep."

Love stretched and walked over to Drake. Wrapping her arms around his shoulders, she kissed him. "Want to watch TV or do me?"

Drake smirked. "I'd love to do you, but I'm going to choose sleep." He smacked her lightly on her butt, and disappeared up the stairs.

Sleep wasn't even an option. A feeling of dread took over as she wondered what had happened to Drake to pull away from her.

Later on, Love stuffed Drake's tuxedo pants in a bag. She'd decided to take his suit to the cleaners when she took her dress. He'd already left for his afternoon shift.

She racked her brain trying to think about everything that happened at the ball. But nothing seemed out of the ordinary. She was tempted to talk to El. Maybe he'd be able to shed some light on things. But she didn't want to involve anyone else. Her mother had once told her not to bring other people into her relationships. Whatever happened between her and Drake was between them.

Shaking her head to clear her mind, she checked the pockets and heard the crinkle of paper from the inside pocket. She pulled an envelope out and noted the return address: Johns Hopkins. The urge to open the envelope reared its ugly head. Love wasn't the type to spy on her man.

She reasoned with herself about it. Drake *had* been acting strange, ever since they'd left the fund-raising event. She was taking his tuxedo to the cleaner and the letter happened to be in his pocket.

Giving in to temptation, she pulled out the contents and scanned them. Her heart dropped. Swallowing hard, she read the letter again.

Johns Hopkins?

She didn't want to jump to conclusions, but her father's words came to mind.

Last I checked, Drake was looking for a career, not a wife.

Love choked back a sob. Had her dad been right all along? Drake had been there, fully vested in their relationship…until the acceptance letter arrived.

You are fundamentally different people. This marriage will be over before it starts.

Pressing a hand against her throat, she considered calling Drake, confronting him with the evidence that he'd lied to her. Except he didn't lie, he'd omitted.

Mark my words, you'll end up heartbroken when he wakes up one morning and realizes he wants more.

Her father's words still stung, because Love had known it was a possibility, even then. But she'd chosen to believe Drake when he said he wanted to be with her, that he loved her.

Love stuffed the letter back in the envelope and set it on Drake's pillow. He'd see it when he got home and have no choice but to mention it. She heard the door shut downstairs and figured the conversation was going to happen sooner rather than later.

When Drake entered the room, she asked him, "What are you doing back so soon?"

"I forgot I don't have a lecture this morning. I figured I chill out with you for a while." He walked over to her, leaned in and kissed her. "Want to get some lunch?"

She shook her head. "No."

Frowning, he asked, "Are you okay?"

"I was… I was going to take your tux to the cleaners." She picked up the envelope from his pillow and held it out. "This was in the pocket."

Drake lowered his gaze.

"Were you going to tell me that you got accepted to Johns Hopkins? Or were you just going to leave without telling me?"

Sighing, he sat down on the edge of the bed. "It's not what you think."

"Isn't it? You've been distant. And then I see this. What am I supposed to think? I've been asking you for days if everything is all right. You've been lying to me for days. I thought we were working toward something here."

"Love, I was going to tell you."

"After you accepted the offer?"

"I haven't accepted the offer. I'm not going to."

"Why? You've wanted this for years. Why wouldn't you take it?"

"Because… I love you. I'm not going to just leave."

"But you considered it."

"Of course I did. It's Johns Hopkins."

"Take it."

His eyes widened. "Love, I'm not taking it."

"Please do."

The fact that the minute she read the letter, she'd immediately thought the worst about Drake didn't sit right with her. It was indicative of a greater problem.

Lack of trust. She'd been burned before, and she didn't want to get hurt again.

"Don't do this," he said. "Don't push me away because you're scared."

"I don't know why I thought we could do this, Drake. All I know is if we continue, I might wind up hating you. It's bad enough that because of me you're turning down a job you've always wanted. And I'm not willing to do another long-distance relationship. Bottom line, my dad was right. We want different things. It's good that we know that now."

"What?" Drake jumped up, staggered back a few steps. "I can't even believe you're going to use your dad's words against me. I'm not that guy. I'm not him. I would never hurt you."

"You wouldn't try. And I love you for that. But I think it's best we end this now, before we ruin each other." Love walked into the bathroom and slammed the door.

Drake pounded on it. "Love."

He kept knocking, calling her name, begging her to talk to him. But Love just leaned against the panel and cried silently.

Drake knocked on the door, waited until he heard "come in" before opening it.

Dr. Leon was seated at his desk. "Drake. What brings you here?"

"I wanted to believe that you'd get over it, that you'd accept me." Drake paced the office. After Love had barricaded herself in the bathroom, he'd stormed out and driven around, turning everything over in his mind.

It was curious timing, receiving the acceptance letter from Johns Hopkins. Almost too coincidental. Then it made sense. His own father hand-delivered the letter, the same day Love's father apologized and asked for forgiveness...? A call to the admissions office confirmed his suspicions. His father had worked with hers, sending over glowing recommendations to their friends at Johns Hopkins, calling in a few favors, and voila!

Drake had just left his dad. He'd yelled at him, not just about this, but about everything that he'd ever done to hurt him. And like every other time his father felt like his back was against the wall, he'd responded in kind. It had been a waste of time, talking to someone who didn't know how to listen. Instead of arguing with him any longer, Drake had walked away and now he found himself staring at the man that he'd *thought* was better than his father.

"I don't know what problem you have with me, but I would have never hurt your daughter. I love her too much. I wanted a life with her, and I was willing to give that fellowship up for her. But I guess I should congratulate you. Because of your interference, your manipulations, she ended it. You got your wish. Your daughter will not be married to me much longer. Maybe she can take that asshole Derrick back so he can cheat on her again."

"Drake," Dr. Leon said.

"No, you don't have to say anything. I'm going to Baltimore. Love made the decision for me. You're happy, huh?"

"Drake—"

"Tell me something." Drake hung his head, took

a deep breath and faced Dr. Leon. "When did you start hating me so much? What did I ever do to you? I thought we were better than that. You were more important to me than my own father."

"I don't hate you."

"Then what is it?" Drake threw his arms out in frustration. "Why?"

"You were right. Love was right. I look at you and I see myself. And my protective instincts kicked in. I didn't want my daughter to fall in love with someone like me."

Drake let out a strained snicker.

"It doesn't mean that I don't care about you, son. I do. I still think this may be the best thing for both of you. This way you can follow your dream. You worked hard for it."

His dream. Yes, he had dreamed of a Johns Hopkins fellowship, followed by a prolific career. But now a woman dominated his dreams. And his every thought.

"Great," he said with no emotion in his tone. "Just so you know, though. None of that matters to me."

Chapter 18

Love was miserable, and it was all her fault. She'd been so scared of being hurt that she'd hurt herself in the process. Drake had told her that he wasn't going to take the job, had begged her to listen to him, but no… She couldn't hear him past the roaring in her brain. The truth was she'd been happier with Drake, as his wife, than she'd ever been in her life. It was like she'd been looking through a peephole for her entire life, but when he kissed her, when he loved her, it was like he'd opened up the window to her soul. Who knew that her best friend would be the man she wanted to spend the rest of her life with?

Then she had to go and mess it up. She'd sent Drake packing when it was the last thing she wanted to do. The worst part? He'd actually left, walked out of her life.

Love had always made fun of silly women who

took to bed after a breakup. She'd thought that would never be her, until it was. Dr. Lovely Grace Washington was licking her wounds, eating cookies and ice cream bars and potato chips—and nothing else. All junk food, all day. The last time she'd looked at herself in the mirror, her hair was a mass of naps on her head, she had chocolate on the corner of her mouth and crud in her eyes. That was yesterday. She could only imagine what she looked like today.

She'd tried to rationalize it. Drake was her longest friend; they'd cut their teeth together. She had every right to mourn the end of their relationship, especially since it could also be the end of the friendship. Love complicated things. *Love sucks*. Pun intended.

It had been three days and his smell still lingered on her pillow, the soft scent of wood and leather. She burrowed her nose into the cotton and closed her eyes. It was distinctively Drake and one whiff made her feel safe and secure, like he always had.

Being with Drake, being loved by him, was like a Pandora's box. She'd let him into places she didn't realize she had. He'd opened up a part of her that was under lock and key. It was magical and terrifying at the same time. How could she live without that? She loved him so much, she literally felt an ache low in her belly.

She checked her phone every minute, hoping to see a message from him. Even a one-word text would be okay. The first day, after she'd told him it was over, they'd run into each other at the hospital. He'd brushed past her, going out of his way to avoid eye contact, acting almost as if she was contagious.

During morning rounds, he'd busied himself talking to a first year resident with big boobs and a huge crush on him. Love wanted to choke her. She couldn't avoid the whispers, the stares. Everyone was speculating the worst—that he'd cheated on her, which couldn't be further from the truth. So she'd called in sick the next two days. She was a coward.

Lana had texted her, phoned her, then finally burst into her room last night. Her cousin ordered her to "get her ass out of that bed," but Love simply rolled over and turned up the television. Eventually, Lana relented, giving her another day to sulk before she called in the big dogs. Not that Love knew who the "big dogs" were. Not even her mother could get her out of her room, and she'd tried countless times.

"Lovely?" *I spoke too soon.*

Gloria limped into the room and sat beside her on the mattress. Love felt bad that she'd basically ignored her mother for two days, especially since she was still a sick woman. Love wanted to be there for her. Tomorrow. Yes, she'd get up and go to work tomorrow.

Familiar hands massaged her shoulders, rubbed her back. "You have to get out of this bed. You've been in here for two days."

"I will, Mom. I'll get up tomorrow."

Gloria let out a heavy sigh. "Your father called."

"I don't want to talk to him." She was pissed at her dad.

After Drake moved out, her father had called and asked her for forgiveness. Confused, Love had played along, asked him why he did it, as if she knew what "it" was. She had no idea what he was talking about. When he'd confessed to coaxing the admissions department at Johns Hopkins to consider Drake for the fellowship, her anger had soared to new heights. It was the first and only time she'd ever cursed at her father, then she'd hung up on him.

"You may not believe him, but he is sorry."

Love looked at her mother. "Why are you defending him, Mom? He doesn't deserve that from you."

Gloria tapped her foot on the carpet. "Love, what happened between me and Leon wasn't all his fault. You know that? It takes two people to make a marriage work and two people to destroy it."

"That doesn't make any sense. One person can ruin a relationship." She should know. She'd just done it. "He cheated on you, Mother."

"Yes, and that sucked. But our marriage was over a long time before he cheated. We just hadn't made it official, because of you."

Love gasped. "What? You two seemed so happy."

"Because that's what we wanted you to believe, babe. Sometimes a relationship is not meant to last a lifetime. Talk about two people whose lives were going in different directions. We grew apart. By the time he cheated on me, I'd already fallen out of love with him. I was just biding my time."

The revelation shocked Love to her core. She'd blamed her dad for being a cheating jerk. Well, he still was a cheating jerk.

"When I talked to him today," Gloria continued, sweeping a cookie crumbs and empty Fruit Snacks wrappers into her hand and throwing them into the small wastebasket beside the bed, "I told him to forgive himself, because I already did. Your father isn't a bad person. He's just misguided."

"And controlling," Love added.

"Very. But his heart was in the right place. He was really worried about you. He apologized to Drake."

Hearing that he'd done so meant a lot to Love. She was sure it made Drake feel better.

"I did light into him, though."

Love wiped a tear from her cheek. "Why did he do it?"

"I'm not even sure he knows. I think what it boils down to is you're his baby girl. No one will be good enough for you in his eyes. All he sees is the potential for hurt, and when you were born he made a vow to never let anyone hurt you."

"*He* hurt me. He manipulated me and my marriage."

"I know. There's no excuse for his behavior, but I do believe he's sincere in his apology."

"I love Drake, Mom. I want him to be happy, have everything he wants. Marriage and kids were never on his must-have list. It was stupid to even get involved, but we went in at full speed instead of being cautious. Now look at us. Barely speaking, barely friends. I hurt him."

She'd heard the tears in his voice as he'd begged her to open the door for him that morning it all fell apart. And she'd stubbornly refused, thinking she was doing what was best for both of them.

Gloria squeezed her hand, pulled her into a tight hug. "I know you. I know Drake. You'll always be friends. It's awkward and hurts now, but it won't be like this always. All is not lost."

Love wasn't so sure. She wanted to believe their friendship could survive. They were stupid to try and change the dynamic so fast. They hadn't thought it through, and they would suffer for the rest of their lives.

"Listen." Gloria pulled Love to her feet, patted her crunchy hair. "You need to get out of this bed and take a shower. You are ripe, daughter."

Love laughed. "I bet you've been waiting to say that since yesterday."

"I have, but I figured I'd give you some time before I pulled rank." Her mother held her face in her hands. "You and Drake need to talk before he leaves the state. I spoke with him yesterday and he's flying to Baltimore today to look for a place. His flight leaves at three o'clock. Now, if you want this friendship that you care about so much, go get him before he leaves."

Her mother was right. She couldn't let Drake leave without telling him she loved him. He had been so much of her world, a huge part of her life. They'd done everything together, been with each other through every life moment that mattered. And one thing stayed constant. They never gave up on each other. She had to get to him.

Love picked up her phone and dialed his number. No answer. Muttering a curse, she hung up and dialed again. It went straight to voice mail. *Damn.*

"Mother." Love ran into the bathroom and started the shower. "Want to ride with me? I have to get to Drake."

Gloria grinned and clapped. "I'm so glad you actually listened to me for once."

Love hugged her. "I love you. I don't know what I would have done if you hadn't been here."

"Lovely, I'll always be here for you. Can I plan that reception now? I've been itching to get started on it."

Love laughed and shook her head at her persistence. "Fine, Mother. If Drake takes me back, you can plan anything you want. I'll be down in ten minutes."

But it was only nine minutes later that Love was speeding toward Drake's apartment, cutting through traffic like a madwoman. He lived in a huge apartment by Interstate 94, far from the hospital, which was why he was at her house, eating up her food, more often than not.

She arrived at the apartment and let out a huge sigh of relief that his car was still parked in his spot under the carport.

Love parked haphazardly in one of the visitor's parking spots outside his place.

Wasting no time, she jumped out of her vehicle. "I'll be back, Mom."

"I'll wait here," Gloria said.

Love ran to the private outdoor entrance to his unit. But when she raised her hand to knock, the door swung open and she tumbled inside.

Drake grabbed her waist, steadying her. Just that contact made her stomach tighten and goose bumps spread up her arms.

"Love?" he asked. "What are you doing here?"

El stepped out from behind him. "Well, well, well. You came. I thought I was going to have to go over and coordinate an intervention." She quickly realized that El was the "big guns" Lana had referred to.

Love winced, her gaze darting back and forth between the two men. Her husband was a sight for sore eyes, dressed in dark jeans and a pale blue button-down shirt. He looked good. She leaned in to catch a whiff of his cologne.

"Did you just smell him?" El asked, amusement flickering in his eyes.

Drake shot him a sideways glance. "Can you leave us alone?"

"Not before I say this. You two need to get it together." He turned from Drake to Love. "You made it here first. We were on our way to your place."

She drew in a sharp breath, meeting Drake's gaze. "You were?"

He nodded.

El slipped out and joined her mother, who was now standing outside Love's car watching everything unfold. "Fix it," he yelled over his shoulder as he crossed to Gloria.

Love smiled sheepishly. "I guess they're sick of us, huh?"

"Pretty much."

Love motioned toward the inside of the apartment. "Can we sit down?"

He wordlessly led her in. Drake's apartment was modern, as opposed to the traditional style of her condo. He didn't like clutter, so there was very little furniture in his place, only what he needed. The pieces were was sleek, the design clean, the colors neutral, with only a flash of color here and there.

It had been months since she'd been at his place. She picked up a throw pillow as she sat on the sofa with him. "I like this," she said lamely.

"You bought it."

"Oh," she said with a quick roll of her eyes. Deciding that now was the time, she added, "I wanted to catch you before you went to Baltimore. I feel like we need to talk, sort things out."

"I'm not going to Baltimore."

Her eyes snapped to his and her heart raced. "Really?"

"I turned them down."

Love smiled and tears filled her eyes. "I… Why?"

"You know why."

"But you gave your resignation at the hospital."

"Your dad offered me my position back. He called this morning, apologized to me for interfering."

"I know." She still couldn't believe her father actually apologized to Drake. Especially since he rarely admitted when he was wrong. "I'm shocked."

"I know, right?"

Love picked at her pants, focused on the corner of the rug. Basically she looked everywhere but at Drake. "I'm glad you didn't take the job."

"Why?"

She met his gaze then, and didn't look away. "I want you to stay. I want to work this out."

Drake let out a shaky breath. Over the past few days, he'd imagined this conversation a million times. Except he'd always thought he'd be the one making the overtures. But now his wife was at his house, telling him that she wanted to be with him.

"I realize how wrong I was," she said. "That I can trust this. I can trust my feelings for you, and yours for me. Because they've always been there. I was just afraid."

"Of me?"

"Of us."

"And you're not anymore?"

She shook her head. "I want you to get rid of your apartment, and let's make this official."

A smile tugged at his lips. "Are you proposing to me?"

Laughing nervously, she shrugged. "Would you accept?"

He stared at her, marveled at the way she nibbled on her lip. When he inhaled, she smelled like lilacs and peaches. "What do *you* think?"

"I don't know. I mean, I want to hear what you have to say. You're just staring at me."

He hooked a hand around her head and pulled her into a kiss. She slid her arms around his neck, pressing herself against him and melting in his embrace. It felt good having her in his arms again.

She drew away first. "Is that your final answer?"

Drake chuckled. "If you'd seen me over the past few days, then you'd know it is."

He'd been the "asshole of the century" according to his little sister. She'd overheard the fight between him and his father, and tried to be there for Drake. Unfortunately, she'd caught the brunt of his anger because she was the closest. He'd eventually run her away, but not before she gave him a piece of her mind and punched him in the arm.

Love had been stuck in his head like a melody. Many times he'd been tempted to drive to her house and lock her in the room until they figured everything out, but he'd always convinced himself to leave it be. And now that she was sitting in front of him, putting her heart on the line, he realized that him moving to Baltimore without her would have never worked, anyway. She'd made it clear that she wanted to complete her residency in Ann Arbor a while ago. There was no way he would have been able to live without her. He was hers for the taking.

"Marry me, Love."

Her mouth fell open. "What? We're already married."

"No, for real."

Drake wanted her to have the wedding that she'd always dreamed of, complete with cake, bridesmaids and a white dress that he hoped fitted her like a second skin.

"You're serious?"

"Trust me, I've never been more serious."

She beamed at him, and he closed his eyes to soak in the warmth of her smile. When she looked at him like that, his whole world opened up.

Since she was being honest, he figured he'd tell her some truths. "Love, you're the only one for me. There is no one else that I would rather…get rid of my apartment for."

Love smacked him on the knee playfully. "You're silly."

"I want to say those vows again, in front of our family and friends, sober. And I want to have a redo of our wedding night, sober." He picked up her hand, brushed his lips against her fingertips, over her palm, then her wrist. Then he pulled a ring box out of his pocket.

"Drake?"

He swallowed before he opened it. The ring he'd purchased in Vegas had been sitting in his safe since they'd arrived home. It was time that she wore it. Slipping it on her finger, he kissed it before he kissed her.

"I love you," he murmured.

"I love you more." She winked. "Yes, I'll marry you again, in front of everybody and their mamas."

They stood, and he pulled her into another kiss.

"Drake," she panted a long while later, tearing her mouth away from his. "We can't do this here. My mom is waiting outside. El is, too. Let's finish this later."

"Hopefully, not too much later." He nibbled on her earlobe.

"You're crazy."

"You love it."

"Oh. One thing," she said, holding up her index finger.

Frowning, he asked, "What?"

"You can't ever leave again."

Drake let his gaze travel over his wife's face. "You don't have to worry about that. I won't."

"Good."

"Good."

She slid her hand into his, lacing their fingers together. "Let's go, then."

Epilogue

One month later, Drake and Love renewed their vows in front of their families and friends. Both fathers were in attendance and on their best behavior, and Love's mother had planned an elegant, yet simple reception.

The ceremony was quick, because they'd already gone through that. They'd written their own vows. And Love had cried like a big baby when Drake told her that he'd follow her anywhere, go through anything, as long as she was with him. There was no minister, just them talking to each other as if there was no one else in the room.

When he'd kissed her, the crowd roared with applause—until Gloria muttered "stop" under her breath, three times.

It was a memorable day, filled with laughter and

tears. Once everyone left, Drake whisked her away to their honeymoon in Saint Thomas, paid for by Dr. Law. It was, according to him, the least he could do.

They'd spent the first hour making love on their private beach, which had always been a fantasy of hers. And they'd just returned to their suite from dinner.

Love stood outside on the hotel balcony, letting the sea breeze caress her face. Weddings were fun and everything, but she never wanted to do that again. Between floral arrangements, caterers, invitations and color schemes, she was exhausted. But she wouldn't have changed anything for the world.

"Where did you go?" Drake asked, stepping outside and sliding his arms around her waist.

Tilting her head back, she kissed his chin. "Just wanted some fresh air. Can you believe we got married—again?"

"Twice within three months. Go figure."

Drake had been her pillar of strength during the hasty planning. She'd come home countless times with tears in her eyes and surrender on her brain. But he'd soothed her, plied her with wet kisses, massages and more.

"Come back to me," he murmured against her mouth. "You're so distracted."

"Just thinking about everything we've been through. It's been a wild few months."

"I wouldn't change a thing."

"Not even one tiny detail?"

He leaned back, eyed her with curiosity. "Are you trying to give me a hint?"

"Well…" She turned in his arms and snaked her

arms around his neck, pulling him down for a quick kiss. "We've been right in front of each other the whole time. Don't you think about what would have happened had we got our heads out of our asses years ago?"

"No." He buried his face in her neck, laved the sensitive skin under her earlobe with his tongue. "I think if we'd discovered this years ago, it would have ruined us. We had to wait for the right place and time."

And that was why she loved him. He was calm, dependable and rationale. And sexy as hell. "Drake?"

"Yes, Love."

"I love you." She yelped when he picked her up and slung her over his shoulder.

He smacked her on her butt, and she laughed with delight. "How about you love me in bed, all night?" Dropping her on the mattress, he bent down, placing a lingering kiss on her swollen lips. "I love you, too… Mrs. Jackson."

* * * * *

KIMANI™
ROMANCE

COMING NEXT MONTH
Available January 16, 2018

#557 HER UNEXPECTED VALENTINE
Bare Sophistication • by Sherelle Green

Nicole LeBlanc lands a coveted gig as lead makeup artist and hairstylist on a series of Valentine's Day commercials. Once she meets the creative director, she's certain he could fulfill her romantic fantasies. Nicole tempts Kendrick Burrstone to take another chance at love…until a media frenzy jeopardizes it all.

#558 BE MY FOREVER BRIDE
The Kingsleys of Texas • by Martha Kennerson

It was like a fairy tale: eloping with Houston oil tycoon Brice Kingsley. Then a devastating diagnosis and a threat from her past forced Brooke Smith Kingsley to leave. Now she can make things right, but only if she can keep her secret—and her distance—from her irresistible husband.

#559 ON-AIR PASSION
The Clarks of Atlanta • by Lindsay Evans

Ahmed Clark left sports to become a radio show host—one who's cynical about romance. But when Elle Marshall goes on air to promote her business, they clash and sizzle over the airwaves. Putting his heart in play is his riskiest move, but it's the only way to win hers…

#560 A TASTE OF DESIRE
Deliciously Dechamps • by Chloe Blake

International real estate agent Nicole Parks isn't expecting romance in Brazil, but she's falling for French vintner Destin Dechamps. Yet he's out to sabotage the deal that will guarantee her a promotion and the adoption she's been longing for. With their dreams in the balance, is there room for love?

Get 2 Free Books,
Plus 2 Free Gifts—
just for trying the
Reader Service!

YES! Please send me 2 FREE Harlequin® Kimani™ Romance novels and my 2 FREE gifts (gifts are worth about $10 retail). After receiving them, if I don't wish to receive any more books, I can return the shipping statement marked "cancel." If I don't cancel, I will receive 4 brand-new novels every month and be billed just $5.69 per book in the U.S. or $6.24 per book in Canada. That's a savings of at least 12% off the cover price. It's quite a bargain! Shipping and handling is just 50¢ per book in the U.S. and 75¢ per book in Canada*. I understand that accepting the 2 free books and gifts places me under no obligation to buy anything. I can always return a shipment and cancel at any time. The free books and gifts are mine to keep no matter what I decide.

168/368 XDN GMWW

Name _____ (PLEASE PRINT)

Address _____ Apt. #

City _____ State/Prov. _____ Zip/Postal Code

Signature (if under 18, a parent or guardian must sign) _____

Mail to the **Reader Service:**
IN U.S.A.: P.O. Box 1341, Buffalo, NY 14240-8531
IN CANADA: P.O. Box 603, Fort Erie, Ontario L2A 5X3

Want to try two free books from another line?
Call 1-800-873-8635 or visit www.ReaderService.com.

*Terms and prices subject to change without notice. Prices do not include applicable taxes. Sales tax applicable in NY. Canadian residents will be charged applicable taxes. Offer not valid in Quebec. This offer is limited to one order per household. Books received may not be as shown. Not valid for current subscribers to Harlequin® Kimani™ Romance books. All orders subject to approval. Credit or debit balances in a customer's account(s) may be offset by any other outstanding balance owed by or to the customer. Please allow 4 to 6 weeks for delivery. Offer available while quantities last.

Your Privacy—The Reader Service is committed to protecting your privacy. Our Privacy Policy is available online at www.ReaderService.com or upon request from the Reader Service.

We make a portion of our mailing list available to reputable third parties that offer products we believe may interest you. If you prefer that we not exchange your name with third parties, or if you wish to clarify or modify your communication preferences, please visit us at www.ReaderService.com/consumerschoice or write to us at Reader Service Preference Service, P.O. Box 9062, Buffalo, NY 14240-9062. Include your complete name and address.

KROM17R3

SPECIAL EXCERPT FROM

It was like something out of a fairy tale: being swept off her feet, then eloping with her one true love, Houston oil tycoon Brice Kingsley. Then a devastating diagnosis and a threat from her past forced Brooke Smith Kingsley to leave the man she loved. Now she has a chance to make things right, but only if she can keep her secret—and her distance—from her irresistible husband.

Read on for a sneak peek at
BE MY FOREVER BRIDE, the next exciting
installment in author Martha Kennerson's
***THE KINGSLEYS OF TEXAS** series!*

Brooke opened the door and walked into the office to find Brice seated behind his desk, signing several documents. "Did you forget something, Amy?"

The sound of his voice sent waves of desire throughout her body, just like they had from the first moment they met. She'd missed it… She'd missed him. "It's not Amy, Brice," Brooke replied, closing the door behind her, knowing this conversation wasn't for the public.

Brice dropped his pen, raised his head and sat back in his seat. "Brooke," he said, his face expressionless.

"Do you have a moment for a quick chat?" She tried to project confidence when in reality she was a nervous wreck inside. Her heart was beating so fast she just knew the whole building could hear it.

KPEXP0118

Brice tilted his head slightly to the right and his forehead crinkled. "You tell me after six months of what I thought was a wonderful marriage that you want out. I convince you to give us time to work things out—at least I thought I had—and go out for your favorite seafood only to come back to find that you've left me with a note." He leaned forward slightly. "You disappear for three months, only communicating through your lawyer, and now you want to chat." His tone was hard but even.

"I…I—"

"Sure, please have a seat." His words were laced with disdain and sarcasm.

Brooke moved forward on unsteady legs, reaching for the support of a chair. She swallowed hard. "You make it sound so—"

"So what? Honest? Is that not what happened?"

"I didn't want to fight. Not then and certainly not now," she explained, trying to hold his angry glare.

"What *do* you want, Brooke?" Brice asked, sitting back in his chair.

"It's simple. I'd like to get through these next several weeks as painlessly as possible. We're both professionals with a job to do."

Brice sat up in his chair. "That we are." He reached into his desk drawer and pulled out a manila envelope. "We can start by you signing the settlement papers so the lawyers can move forward with the divorce."

Don't miss BE MY FOREVER BRIDE
by Martha Kennerson, available February 2018
wherever Harlequin® Kimani Romance™
books and ebooks are sold!

KPEXP0118

Want to give in to temptation with
steamy tales of irresistible desire?

Check out **Harlequin® Presents®,
Harlequin® Desire** and
Harlequin® Kimani™ Romance books!

New books available every month!

CONNECT WITH US AT:

Harlequin.com/Community

 Facebook.com/HarlequinBooks

Twitter.com/HarlequinBooks

Instagram.com/HarlequinBooks

Pinterest.com/HarlequinBooks

ReaderService.com

**ROMANCE WHEN
YOU NEED IT**

PGENRE2017

LOVE
Harlequin
romance?

Join our Harlequin community to share your thoughts and connect with other romance readers!

Be the first to find out about promotions, news, and exclusive content!

Sign up for the Harlequin e-newsletter and download a free book from any series at **www.TryHarlequin.com**

**ROMANCE WHEN
YOU NEED IT**

HSOCIAL2017